the Dessert Diaries

Kiki Takes the CAKE

by Laura Dower

Raintree is an imprint of Capstone Global Library Limited, a company incorporated in England and Wales having its registered office at 264 Banbury Road, Oxford, OX2 7DY – Registered company number: 6695582

www.raintree.co.uk
myorders@raintree.co.uk

Edited by Kristen Mohn
Designed by Philippa Jenkins
Original illustrations © 2017 Capstone Global Limited Library
Illustrated by Lilly Lazuli
Production by Kathy McColley
Originated by Capstone Global Limited Library
Printed and bound in China.

ISBN 978 1 4747 2214 8
20 19 18 17 16
10 9 8 7 6 5 4 3 2 1

British Library Cataloguing in Publication Data
A full catalogue record for this book is available
from the British Library.

All the Internet addresses (URLs) given in this book were valid at the time of going to press. However, due to the dynamic nature of the Internet, some addresses may have changed, or sites may have changed or ceased to exist since publication. While the author and publisher regret any inconvenience this may cause readers, no responsibility for any such changes can be accepted by either the author or the publisher.

Contents

Autumn delight

Home
Meet the bakers
Recipes
- Cakes
- Cookies
- Tray bakes
- Breads
- Gluten free
- Vegan
- Dairy free
- Other

Archive
- January
- February
- March

Hello, Sweeties!

As always, a great big sugar-coated thank you for supporting the bakery these past several months. In a big city, it's sometimes hard to stand out and get the attention we crave. But so far, things have been pretty sweet. We're so glad to welcome repeat visitors who keep coming back to try all the new things we have to offer.

Which brings me to the point of today's blog: AUTUMN OFFERINGS! This month at Daisy's Desserts we're experimenting with pumpkin and spice and other autumn flavours. Some of the cool items you'll see on our seasonal menu:

Pumpkin Cheesecake Pops

Harvest Biscuits with Cranberries
and Orange Zest

Baked Pear Pudding Tart

Pumpcakes

Honeycross Buns

In addition to food for every autumn mood, the crew at Daisy's now has crayons and colouring books available for the artistically inclined. And if there's a sweet treat you've been wanting to try, or if you have a suggestion to make Daisy's even better, just let us know! Remember: your taste buds are my best buds. I'm always happier when I see customers with crumbs on their shirts.

Happy autumn, everyone!

xo, Daisy

Piece of cake

"Any volunteers to tackle these questions?" Mr Galipeau asked the science class, impatiently tapping his ruler on the white board.

Does baking a cake make a chemical change or physical change?

Does the quantity or order of ingredients affect the reaction?

If you bake a fudge cake vs a carrot cake, does it make a difference in the reaction?

Kiki Booker raised her hand high. She shifted in her seat and toyed with the plaits on her head.

"Does anyone besides Kiki want to explain this for me?" the teacher asked. "Mr Lopez?"

Eduardo Lopez rubbed his buzz-cut. "Uh, Mr G., can't you give us a hint? All this problem is doing is making me hungry."

"As usual," Mr G. said and turned to a red-haired girl sitting way in the back. "Maggie? How about you?"

The girl shrugged. "I'm not totally sure, Mr Galipeau," she said. "Is it a chemical change?"

"Yes, Ms McAllister!" he said enthusiastically. "Now tell me more."

But Maggie just gave him a blank stare.

Kiki's hand was still up. Kiki loved cake, and she loved science. She was absolutely bursting to give the answers.

Mr G. turned back to Kiki and let out a sigh. "Okay, Ms Booker, why don't you explain to the class what you think I'm looking for?"

Kiki cleared her throat. How was it possible that no one else had a clue? These questions were, well, a *piece of cake.* "When you bake," she began, "every ingredient has a different job. Flour is the base. Baking powder makes the cake fluffy. Eggs, which are not a liquid or a solid but a *colloid*, are like the glue that binds everything together. Sugar makes it sweet, of course."

Mr Galipeau smiled and nodded. "Go on."

"Mixing dry and wet ingredients," Kiki continued, "has to be done in a certain order so the ingredients respond – or react – the way they need to. The proteins in flour bond and make gluten. The baking powder releases carbon dioxide, which makes the batter bubble. The bubbles make the cake expand. The heat in an oven turns the goopy batter, which is another colloid, into something solid ..."

"How do you *know* all these things?" someone whined from the back.

Kiki smiled. This lover of all things baked was on a *roll.* "I like cake, okay?" she joked. "Anyway, I haven't even got to the best part ..."

"Okay, Ms Booker," Mr Galipeau interrupted.

"Let's give some other pupils a chance to speak. Does anyone else have anything to add?"

Eduardo's hand shot up.

"I wanna know what the question said: What's the difference between fudge and carrot cake, besides the gross factor? I mean, who would put vegetables in a cake?"

Everyone in class laughed. But Mr Galipeau turned to Kiki again. "Ms Booker?"

Kiki flipped her plaits. "Totally. So, obviously those kinds of cakes are different because they have different ingredients. Putting carrots in a cake can make it denser. And the texture can change if you don't add liquid gradually, or if you mix too long. And ..."

"Okay, time to wrap up," Mr Galipeau said.

"*Psssst,*" said the boy sitting directly behind Kiki. "Do you memorize the textbook or what?"

Of course that voice had permission to tease. It belonged to Kiki's best pal, Jesse Gordon. When Kiki looked back at Jesse, he swished his brown fringe back with a flick of his head. "Brainiac!" he mouthed the words and stuck out his tongue comically.

Kiki didn't mind. He was just being Jesse. Some people thought it was funny that her closest friend was a boy, and hilarious that he happened to be the coolest boy in the whole year. But Kiki and Jesse had bonded way back in nursery school over play dough and lollies, and they'd been inseparable ever since.

Unlike Kiki, Jesse was no science whizz, but he was clever. He teased her because he couldn't help himself. He was born a practical joker.

Kiki rolled her eyes at Jesse and turned back to the teacher.

"That brings us to this month's project. I want you all to think more about chemical and physical reactions in the kitchen. Are you ready for a little food chemistry?" Mr Galipeau passed out a yellow sheet of paper.

Molecules in Motion

Changing State: Evaporation, Condensation, Freezing or Melting

Forming a Precipitate

The Rate of a Chemical Reaction: temperature, catalysts, chemical change

Using Chemical Change to Identify an Unknown: endothermic vs exothermic

Energy Changes in Chemical Reaction: pH and colour changes

"I want you to look over this list carefully. During the next few weeks, I want you to experiment in your kitchens. Record your ingredients, measurements and methods. Use these scientific concepts to write a report about how your chosen recipe is prepared. And it has to be edible." Mr Galipeau looked directly at Eduardo.

"Aw, man!" Eduardo complained.

Everyone groaned. They wanted an excuse to eat food – not to write about it. But Kiki was excited. This was *easy*. She could do this work with her eyes super-glued shut.

"The only thing I'll cook up is a disaster," joked Eduardo.

Kiki laughed. "Actually, that'd be cool if you could make a cake that explodes."

A sly grin spread across Eduardo's face. "Or a soup tsunami ..."

Class was interrupted abruptly by the lunch bell. Everyone jumped up from their seats and moved quickly to the door to head downstairs to the canteen. Kiki hurried there too. All that sweet talk had made her absolutely ravenous.

Eyes searching the lunchroom, Kiki found an empty spot and sat down with her tray. She was promptly joined by Jesse and Rob, another boy from Year 7, who belched as he sat down.

"Why are you guys – and all guys – so obnoxious?" Kiki complained.

"Aw, you're just saying that to be nice," Jesse joked.

"Ha! Good one!" Rob snorted.

"We're experts in rude, right?" Jesse said, throwing his arm up for Rob's high-five.

Kiki sighed. "Okay, weirdos."

"Speaking of weird, how's the Brainy Bunch?" Jesse asked with just a touch of snideness.

"What's the Brainy Bunch?" Rob asked, shovelling spaghetti into his mouth.

Kiki frowned. "Stop it, Jesse! Please don't make fun of me or the group. Rob, it's *actually* called the Supernovas. And it's– "

"Out of this world?" Jesse cracked up.

"Remind me why I'm friends with you?" Kiki asked with a groan.

"Oh, you know I'm kidding, Kiki," Jesse said.

And he was. Jesse knew that Kiki's participation in the group was actually very impressive, considering the fact that the Supernovas was a science club for Year 10 pupils.

Kiki had been invited to join because of her high exam results and because she'd won the school science fair for three years running.

Last year she'd won with a project on the decomposition of school lunches. It was actually quite scandalous – the canteen servers weren't too happy about the mould Kiki discovered in the macaroni and cheese vats! The year before that, Kiki investigated bacteria all over the school – on lockers, door handles, stair railings – which led to a new rules for cleaners. Kiki went the distance for every big idea. Often, Kiki's research led to actual *change*. The canteen workers and cleaners might not have loved her, but teachers did.

But unlike most teachers, the members of the Supernovas didn't warm up to Kiki straight away. They treated her like she was the little sister at the end of the table who gets ignored during the entire meal. And, in fact, she *was* a little sister. Her older brother Shawn was in Year 11 and served as an advisor to the group – at least he did until he got too busy with rugby practice.

It wasn't until one meeting in the canteen that the Supernovas started to pay attention to the new member. When Kiki concocted a seasoning out of ground up cheesy puffs for the group's chips, the club members *really* began to appreciate Kiki's on-the-spot skills – as well as her talent for truly "useful" science.

The Supernovas typically met twice a month. Sometimes they just did homework, which Kiki thought was great because she got to hear about the chemistry, physics or biology that the older pupils were working on. Sometimes the group competed in local science fairs, and Kiki (a science fair champ, after all) learned a lot from listening to the other members share their passions about absolute zero or surprising sources of global warming. Sometimes the club just sat around and talked about science in the news or an old episode of *The Big Bang Theory*. Kiki loved it all.

One of the pupils in the Supernovas called Bradley always told the coolest stories. He was working with *real* NASA scientists on an experiment with wind turbines. His dad was an engineer and had a connection. Kiki was honoured just to listen to Bradley describe the work he did. She knew that one day she too would be a scientist who did important work. Kiki Booker had big dreams.

"Hey!" Jesse flung a piece of crust at Kiki to get her attention. "Earth to Kiki," Jesse called through cupped hands.

"I was just thinking about the science of lunchroom waste," Kiki joked. "And how we desperately need a dessert intervention for *this*." She held up a teeny dish of dark, soggy-looking fruit cocktail. "Nobody's eating it."

"That's because it's nasty. I mean, come on: It's *beige*. It's probably not even real fruit. Just chemicals. Maybe if they put some chocolate icing on it ..." Jesse said.

"When in doubt, ice it!" Rob cheered.

"I agree. Chocolate icing improves everything." Kiki laughed.

The lunch bell rang and the trio split up. Kiki and Jesse headed for their English lesson.

"What are you doing after school today?" Kiki asked. "Do you want to study together?"

"Football practice," Jesse said with a shake of his head.

"You always have football practice," Kiki said.

"Not true." Jesse jumped from side to side with quick footwork like he was on the field. "Only nearly every day," he joked. "Zip. Zig. Zap!" He bounced around Kiki.

"Show off," Kiki grumbled at his moves.

"Gotta keep up my skills! But I'll study with you tomorrow. Or the day after that."

Kiki shrugged. "It's okay. I know you have other, *more important* things to do than talk about science or books with me." They shared a love of science fiction, but lately they hadn't had much time to discuss their favourite series, *The Lost Tribes*, about a group of children whose parents are scientists on a secret mission.

"What's more important than book talk with you?" Jesse joked. "It's your name, *Booker*! And while we're hanging, we could make a pit stop at this cool new bakery just down the street. They have cookies the size of my face."

"Wait, the size of your face, or the size of your ego?" Kiki teased.

"Not enough dough in the world ..." Jesse joked back. "But seriously, they have struffoli and farfennussen and all sorts of sticky, gooey, amazing caramel cookies and sugary cakes with, like, candy floss stuff on top. Yum!"

"What is farfennussen?" Kiki asked. "It sounds like a car."

"Ha! You don't know?" Jesse wailed. "I gotcha! I know something you don't know!"

"Wait. Do you mean pfeffernuesse?" Kiki asked. "I know *that*. It's a German spice cookie. If you're trying to outsmart me, get the word right."

Jesse rolled his eyes. "How about I just ignore you instead?" he said. He explained how the bakery had just sort of appeared out of nowhere into this old building on the corner in the autumn. One day it was an empty hardware shop, and the next day it was an eclectic bakery that even played music sometimes. Jesse had been there once or twice with his cousin.

When they sat down at their desks for their English lesson, Kiki could not stop thinking about the fancy pfeffernuesse and all the treats Jesse described. And then, in an even sweeter twist of fate, the class was given a new reading assignment: the first three chapters of *Charlie and the Chocolate Factory*. What were the chances, Kiki wondered?

After school, with no plan to walk with Jesse, Kiki took the bus home. Kiki sat at the front of the bus, near the driver, holding onto the silver pole that ran from the ceiling to the bus floor. The bus passed an enormous construction site with a sign.

Bakery Barn
GRAND OPENING COMING SOON!
900 square metres of delicious!

That must be the place Jesse was talking about, she thought, leaning over to get a better look. But the bus kept moving down the street. Kiki had a flash of recognition and realized she had heard of the place and seen that logo before – at *home*. Dad had some papers lying around that had "Bakery Barn" plastered all over them. That was his new account. He'd been hired by the company to help promote the new shop.

What a funny coincidence! Despite believing that scientific proof was required for pretty much *everything*, Kiki liked coincidences. They took her by surprise and triggered a dozen more what-if questions inside her head.

The bus journey was taking forever, so Kiki settled back with her Roald Dahl book and came across these yummy lines: "*... marshmallows that taste of violets, and rich caramels that change colour every ten seconds as you suck them, and little feathery sweets that melt away deliciously the moment you put them between your lips.*"

Mmmmmm. Kiki's stomach gurgled hungrily at the thought of the caramels.

The only thing better than baking science was magical baking science! Willy Wonka would have been able to solve any chemistry problem assigned from her science class. He was a genius, with his Everlasting Gobstoppers (there was a time-space continuum problem hidden in there somewhere) and river of chocolate (what would the rates of flow and ebb be in that kind of river?).

All this talk about the science of food reminded Kiki that she needed to think about what kitchen chemistry she'd work on for the project in Mr Galipeau's class. It wasn't really a big deal, but as always, she wanted to choose something impressive. She was well beyond most Year 7 pupils already, but that wasn't enough for Kiki.

Roald Dahl was good inspiration. So were the Supernovas. Whatever she did when it came to science, Kiki kept her eyes on the prize. She had to come up with something great.

When the bus finally arrived at her stop, Kiki exited the side door and headed for her flat. She took the lift up to the top floor where her family lived. Shawn wouldn't be home because of rugby practice on the other side of the city. Kiki turned the key in the lock, then stepped inside and re-locked the front door.

"Hello?" she called out of habit. As she suspected, no one was home except for her two turtles, Honey and Molasses, and they didn't talk much.

Kiki's mum had left a note on the kitchen worktop.

Kiki and Shawn,

Dad home v. v. late tonight. I'm at class late too. Pls. defrost creamed curry chicken and peel carrots.

Love ya, Mum

Kiki found the creamed chicken in a clear container in the freezer. It was marked and measured, just like every meal. Mum loved to cook. One look inside the freezer was evidence of this: various containers with taped labels and dates for an entire week's worth of meals – most of them Jamaican-inspired, like jerk beef patties or oxtail soup.

After setting the chicken dish on the worktop, Kiki grabbed a snack – lemon yogurt with a little flax seed on top. She dropped a lettuce leaf into Honey and Molasses's turtle terrarium and headed for the den. No sooner was Kiki seated with her homework than her mobile phone rang.

"Hey, is this Kiki?" Bradley from the Supernovas was calling to see if Kiki would be around for an emergency meeting the next afternoon.

"An emergency meeting?" Kiki gulped. That sounded serious. "What's the big deal?"

"We submitted an entry to be on the *FTS Show*, and we were chosen to compete!"

"*FTS*?" Kiki gasped. "I love that programme!" *FTS* stood for Future of Tech and Science, and it was on Tuesdays and Thursdays. Really clever children from all over the city competed, mostly for bragging rights, although there was a special gift card prize for the club that won first place in any competition.

"This is actually the first time they're inviting most of the city science clubs to all go head-to-head," Bradley went on. "We need four members to compete officially."

"And you want ... *me*?"

"Yeah. With me we've got three people committed, but everyone else is having schedule issues because there's some band competition going on that same day. Could you be our fourth?"

"Me?" Kiki repeated into the phone a little too enthusiastically. "You really want *me*?"

"Yes, you. We're meeting tomorrow at this new bakery ..." Bradley explained.

"Bakery Barn?"

"Nah, it's called Daisy's Desserts. Pretty cool place, if you ask me. They let you sit there and eat cookies and stay for hours if you want. It's a perfect meeting spot. And it's right down the street from the school. You can't miss it."

"Wow." Kiki smiled to herself. *This* must be the

same bakery that Jesse told her about. Between Daisy's Desserts and Bakery Barn, the science assignment and the Willy Wonka book, the universe was definitely sending a sign that Kiki needed to be eating more cookies. "Are you sure you really want me?" she asked Bradley again.

"*Yes*," Bradley said, chuckling. "No offence, but we can't actually do this without you. If you don't show up, we'll be short a player and won't be able to compete."

"Oh," Kiki sighed. "I get it. I'm sort of your last resort, huh?"

She wanted so desperately to imagine that the reason the Supernovas had asked her to compete was because she was the brainiest of all. But the truth was something a little bit different.

"So, tomorrow at Daisy's Desserts?" Bradley repeated. "Right after school?"

"I'll be there," Kiki said before hanging up.

So what if she wasn't the team's first choice, if she was just a fill-in? It was okay. She didn't plan to be "the last resort" for very long! This was Kiki's chance to prove just how clever she was.

Chapter 2

Shawn and the sticky bun

"So you're meeting at the bakery about *what?*" Jesse asked as he and Kiki walked together.

"They want me to be on their team for the *FTS Show!*"

Jesse stopped short. "No way. My dad watches that programme all the time. He always tries to get me to watch with him. I think he hopes the science-love thing will rub off on me."

"Maybe if it were the *Future of Tech and Science FICTION*, he'd get you to watch," Kiki teased. "I am so excited. And meeting at a bakery is so cool, right? Off school grounds. Like I'm really one of them, not just some pathetic Year 7 pupil."

"I have to be honest, it would almost be worth being a Supernova to get a free ginormous cookie at the club meeting."

"But then you'd have to stop making fun of us, and you wouldn't have anything left to joke about," Kiki said.

"Speaking of jokes, you know the name of your group stinks, right? I'd rename it something else."

"What's wrong with Supernovas?" Kiki asked. "It describes us perfectly. We're *stars*!"

"Yeah, an exploding star that's about to die out," Jesse said.

"Oh, shut up. They're still cool."

Jesse smiled. "I'm just kidding, Keeks. You know I think it's cool that you're in the Brainy Bunch. I guess since I'm not in your club, I'll have to get one of my own mega cookies – or better yet, one of Daisy's double delight brownies."

"Is there anything on their menu you haven't tried?" Kiki asked.

"I'm working my way through it. We are talking

seriously grade-A+ pastries," Jesse said. "And here we are!"

Kiki looked up to see a shimmer of lights decorating a quaint shopfront. A red awning with golden letters shone in the sun.

Kiki and Jesse raced up to the large front door. Kiki pressed her face to the frosted glass and then pushed the door open. A gush of warm, delicious air hit as they moved inside.

"Wow, it smells so good in here," Kiki said, inhaling deeply. The whole place smelled like yummy burnt sugar, cherries, marshmallow, peaches and lemons: Kiki couldn't quite make out any *single* smell. As soon as she was sure she smelled one thing, another wonderful smell popped into her nose. She just knew it all smelled *good*.

Kiki couldn't believe how many people were in the shop in the middle of the afternoon, buzzing from their tables to the counter and then back again. There was a gaggle of mums with buggies, sipping cups of coffee while their children played with toys in one corner of the shop. A cluster of old men huddled together spraying pie crumbs at each other while debating politics with their mouths full of food. A statuesque woman in a leather coat peered over her sunglasses at an array of cupcakes inside a glass cabinet. There were cookies, cakes and pies galore!

"Just wait 'til you taste it," said Jesse. "Pretty amazing, isn't it? Like sugar paradise."

"Minus the coconut trees, of course," Kiki giggled. She wasn't sure why, but she felt a warm tingling sensation in her fingertips, toes and even on the tip of her nose.

"Do you feel that?" she asked Jesse.

"Feel what? My awesomeness?"

"Right," Kiki said, rolling her eyes. Jesse was so full of himself, in the most charming way possible.

The crowds inside Daisy's Desserts swooped in and out. Kiki found herself staring at one particular woman who bounced from table to table. Was she the bakery owner? She had a head of curly red hair poking out from her ponytail and a smile that could light a dark room. Scientifically speaking, she was an exothermic reaction, providing warmth all around. Kiki noticed that every table she approached brightened up at her arrival. She had this *power*. What was that?

Out of the corner of her eye, Kiki spotted the table with the three Supernovas, who were laughing and passing around a giant slice of fudgy cake.

Jesse saluted as he said goodbye. "So they're here, you're here and I'm out. I'll grab my goods to take away so I don't bring down the group IQ." Jess made a goofy face then said, "Later, gator."

"Thanks for walking with me," Kiki said. "And don't forget to do that English homework."

"Do I ever forget to do homework?" Jesse said.

Kiki made a face. "Do you really want me to answer that?"

Jesse laughed and went up to place his order as Kiki headed towards the table with the fudge cake. She didn't take her eyes off its gooey deliciousness.

Of course, if she focused on the cake, she would not have to think about how incredibly nervous she was feeling. At most Supernovas meetings, Kiki sat there quietly, taking it all in, listening to the older members and learning new things. Today, she felt like they might put her – the "extra" – on the spot.

"It's Brainiac Junior," said Sam as he stuffed a forkful of chocolate into his mouth.

"Looks delish," Kiki said meekly as she took the empty chair at the table.

"Sam, are you gonna share that or what?" Bradley asked.

Sam passed the fork to Kiki, but she wrinkled her nose. "Chocolate fudge with a side of shared bacteria, huh?" Kiki cracked. The group laughed and Sam made a show of licking his finger and then digging it right into the cake.

"Eww! That's nasty!" Tamara, a girl with spiky blond hair, said and covered her mouth like she was going to throw up.

They began discussing the *FTS Show*. Kiki

already knew the format. All contestants dressed up in lab coats in different colours. Teams sat up near a podium, taking turns answering science questions in a variety of categories such as technology, biology, chemistry, physics, botany and environmental science.

Bradley showed the group a practice worksheet. Kiki thought the questions looked hard. Maybe too hard?

Maybe I really don't belong here? Kiki worried.

She sat at the table, eyes on the forkful of uneaten chocolate cake, feeling a little bit out of her element. She checked an old-fashioned clock on the wall. A half hour into the meeting and she'd hardly said a word. She was beginning to worry that she was in over her head with this competition. She felt fine when the group met at school, but now, with the contest, it was different. She felt like the Year 7 pupil she was – low brain in the pecking order.

After a little while, the group went over all the important details and handed out the release forms their parents had to sign. They began to gather their things.

"You all have to go?" Kiki asked tentatively.

"Yeah, Bradley and I have practice at the theatre," Tamara said. "And Sam's got something else going on. What about you?" She looked concerned. "Is someone is coming to pick you up?"

"My brother is probably on his way," Kiki said, not sure that he really was.

"Hold up. Hasn't Shawn got rugby practice on the other side of town?" Tamara asked. She was one of Shawn's best pals, so she knew his plans. "Do you wanna use my mobile phone and text him?"

Kiki shook her head. "I texted him a little while ago. I'm okay, thanks. I'm sure he's on his way. I'll just wait here."

"Okay then," Tamara said. "If he doesn't text back soon, let me know. Thanks for helping us out with the *FTS Show*." Tamara wore these cool overalls and a leather jacket, and Kiki couldn't help but stare. Not only was she a super-clever super-girl, but Tamara did not fit the stereotype of most of the other members of the Supernovas. Most of them, Kiki included, appeared to care way more about facts and figures than about their outfits.

Kiki didn't feel like she had much fashion sense. She just wore whatever was comfortable, mostly her collection of science T-shirts, like the one with a colourful periodic table of elements that said *I Wear This Periodically*. Or the one that had a cartoon of an exploding beaker that said *I'm Overreacting*!

Once Tamara left, Kiki checked the clock on the wall again. Shawn really should have been here by now. He had told Kiki that practice would last an hour, and then he'd come to the meeting at Daisy's right away. Had he forgotten? And why wasn't he checking his phone?

"Your friends are gone, huh?"

Kiki looked up and found herself face-to-face with the redheaded woman who'd been buzzing around the shop for the last hour.

"Oh," Kiki said, surprised. "Yeah. They're not

actually my friends. I'm just in this academic club with them. They're in Year 10. I'm only in Year 7."

"You're a clever cookie, then, huh?" she said with a wink.

"Well, I'm going to be in this contest with them, but I think they only chose me because I was available," Kiki tugged nervously on her plait.

"Well, guess what? It takes a team to get things done – a *whole* team," she said with a smile. "I'm Daisy Duncan, baker in charge, and those fine folks over there are part of my team." She pointed to the ladies bustling behind the counter. "That's Babs with the fancy silver 'do, and that's Dina with the long plait and big smile."

Both bakers stopped and waved at Kiki. "They help me out anywhere and everywhere they're needed," Daisy went on. "And Carlos, the big burly bloke over there, *should* be in the back right now, baking up the goods!" Daisy kindly chastised, loudly enough for him to hear.

Carlos laughed and waved his hand dismissively

at her from the corner where he was fixing a display.

Kiki giggled. "I'm Katherine Booker. But everyone calls me Kiki."

"Well, Kiki, did those hungry geniuses share any fudge cake with you? It was the special today."

"I was holding out for my own piece," Kiki said, pointing at the smeary mess of cake left behind on the plate.

"Good call," Daisy said with a laugh and quickly brought another piece.

When Kiki took a big bite with her own very clean fork, she mumbled, "Gooey. *Mmmm!*"

"I take that as the highest compliment!" Daisy laughed. "Gooey is my goal!"

Daisy took a seat next to Kiki and put her chin in her hand, giving Kiki her full attention. "Have you been here before?" she asked. "I don't remember seeing you."

"Not before today," Kiki said, shifting in her chair. It felt like she was on the hot seat, even though this was the coolest place ever. "Do you own this bakery?"

"Yes I do. It's my dream," Daisy said. "Ever since I was a little girl baking in the kitchen with my Nana Belle. She was the *real* baker. A lot of the recipes we've developed came from her old wooden recipe box. I've been baking with my team for years now."

Kiki wanted to hear more about Daisy's story, but she couldn't really focus on the details, because she was worried about her brother. She glanced over at the front door of the bakery. She wasn't allowed to catch the bus home by herself after dark, and the sun had nearly set.

"Are you waiting for someone?" Daisy asked, reading Kiki's mind.

"My brother was supposed to meet me here. But he had rugby practice, and I think maybe he forgot. He's not answering his phone."

Daisy nodded. "Stay as long as you need. I'm sure he'll be here soon. Oh, and by the way – that cake you're eating? It's got a special ingredient in it: courage. So eat up." She smiled and tapped one finger on Kiki's head as she headed back to work.

"Hi, sis!" The door had burst open and a voice came from the front of the shop. Shawn shuffled towards Kiki with his duffel bag across one shoulder. "Come on, Keeks," he said. "We have to go!"

"What happened?" Kiki asked. "I've been waiting here forever. Well, for half an hour anyway."

"Coach kept me late, then the bus broke down and my phone died. Sorry." Shawn beckoned Kiki and turned to leave, but all at once, he stopped short and inhaled deeply.

"Wait. What's that smell?" he said, his eyes lighting up.

Kiki grinned. "I know. Right?"

Daisy swooped back over from the other side of the shop and introduced herself to Shawn. "So you're the rugby star!"

"Yeah, uh ..." Shawn said. "Sorry I was ... wait, who are you again? And *what is that amazing smell*?"

Kiki sniffed at the air. "Chocolate ...?" she guessed.

Shawn shook his head. "Nah, it's more like ..."

"Salted caramel," Daisy said as she handed Shawn a crisp white bag. Inside was a pecan caramel sticky bun.

"My favourite! And I'm starving," Shawn said with a gasp. "How did you know?" He looked at Daisy like she was some kind of magician.

"She just *knows* things," Kiki whispered, nodding as if she and Daisy were old friends.

Somehow, it felt like they were.

Daisy shrugged. "I hope I see the two of you again in my bakery," she said. "Behind every customer there's a special story, and I can't wait to hear yours."

As Daisy walked away and Kiki thanked her for helping out, Shawn was left scratching his head.

Chapter 3

Honey and molasses

"Good morning, Honey," Kiki cooed into the terrarium. "Good morning, Molasses."

As she said their names, Kiki realized that it was no accident she'd named her reptiles after sugary toppings. Here was empirical evidence that Kiki Booker was always thinking about sweets.

Kiki's mother burst into the kitchen holding some wet clothes. "Why are you leaving these on the bathroom floor?" she said to Kiki. "What a waste, mon. Now they need to be rewashed."

Sometimes when Mum was a little bit stressed out, she slipped into Jamaican patois. Kiki and Shawn did too, sometimes, but mostly just for fun.

"I'm sorry!" Kiki said and took the wet laundry. "Breathe easy, Mum. I'll deal with it."

Mum sighed. "Big up yer chest, Kiki," she said, which meant, *Stand tall and take responsibility*. Or, in even plainer terms: *Pick up your mess and don't do it again*. Kiki was great at homework but not always so great about housekeeping.

"Did Shawn tell you that Auntie Pat is coming to stay with us for a little while?" Mum asked. "She's coming from Kingston to help out until I finish my semester." Kiki's mum was already a nurse, but she was taking more classes to become a nurse practitioner.

Kiki smiled. Auntie Pat was the best aunt in the world. She always told great stories about her garden, her goats and the rest of their family in Jamaica.

"Really? That's great! But why?" Kiki asked.

"I can't put all the household things on you children, and your father has more travel coming up, and my course load is about to double ..." Kiki's mum sounded exhausted. "It's only temporary to have Pat here, but, it'll be a huge help. She comes tomorrow night!"

"Can't wait!" Kiki said. "I love Auntie Pat and her curry goat and jerk chicken and – *ooh*, her gizzada!" Gizzada was a Jamaican coconut tart. Kiki hadn't eaten those since Year 5, when she'd visited her mum's home country.

"So go and deal with the washing now and we'll get set," Mum said, nudging Kiki along.

Both Kiki and Shawn were in charge of washing their own clothes. Mum was strict about things like that. In addition to getting near-perfect grades, they were supposed to help prepare meals, wash clothes and help keep the house clean as a conch shell. But two teenagers needed some extra guidance during the busier times. Auntie Pat could help them get back on track.

Kiki's mum gave her daughter a big, strong hug. "How are maths and science going? And the meeting about the science competition?"

"I don't know, Mum. The Supernovas are so clever," Kiki said, after telling her about the meeting. "I'm not sure I can keep up."

Mum tossed her head back and let out a laugh. "You? Keep up? You don't just keep up – you fly past the rest!"

Kiki blushed. "I don't fly past Year 10 pupils, Mum. I, like, doggie paddle next to them."

Her mum laughed again and shook her head. "Kiki, you wouldn't be in the club if you didn't deserve to be there. You know more than you think."

"Where's Dad this morning?" Kiki asked, realizing that her father hadn't turned up in the kitchen as usual to get his coffee and read the paper before work.

"Another crack-of-dawn marketing meeting for the Bakery Barn," Mum said, still buzzing around the kitchen.

"Oh," Kiki poked at her waffles. "Sometimes I feel like I never see you two anymore."

"I know," Mum sighed. "This is why Auntie Pat's

visit will be good for all of us. She'll help out, and we'll organize some more family time. I know Dad misses his long talks about logic problems with you."

Kiki's fondness for maths was inherited. Although Dad wasn't a maths professor or anything fancy like that, he was still a numbers geek. He and Kiki would challenge each other to weekly Sudoku contests. Or at least they had until he got so extra-busy recently.

"Should I warm up some meat pies for lunch today?" Mum asked.

Kiki yawned. "I don't know." She loved Jamaican food, but eating the same thing day in and day out was getting tedious. Auntie Pat would fix that too. "How about peanut butter and jam today?" Kiki asked. "On white bread?"

Mum raised her eyebrows and shrugged. "I guess once in a while you can indulge in non-brain food."

A few moments later, a dishevelled Shawn

dragged himself to the breakfast table and downed three bowls of cereal without even saying a proper good morning. The clock read eight o'clock, so they had to leave. If they missed their bus, they'd be in trouble.

"I'll be late again tonight," Mum warned as Kiki and Shawn headed for the door. "So I'm leaving money for you. Get some takeaway. Pizza is fine."

"Thanks, Mum," Kiki said, giving her a kiss. "Friday night pizza night!"

"Just save me a slice," Mum shouted as they slammed the door behind them.

Kiki and Shawn caught the bus, and Kiki spotted the signs again when they got to the area where Bakery Barn was going to be. The big chicken on the sign looked weird. They were certainly planning a big launch, weren't they? Everywhere she went, Kiki was being stalked by baked goods.

Maybe a clever cake recipe was the perfect choice for the cooking project in Mr Galipeau's class? She could write about the chemical and physical changes that take place, and the endothermic process, in which the cake absorbs energy in the form of heat. But what if everyone chose a cake recipe? She wanted hers to be special.

At school Kiki met up with her friends in the assembly hall before class. Jesse was slouched in a seat, skimming his maths book. She peeked at his notebook to see what unit he was on, since she was in advanced maths. Inverse functions – she loved solving those! Also sitting with Jesse was a girl called Emme who was in their year. She always wore cute character T-shirts and ruffled skirts with coloured tights, making her way more of a fashion plate than Kiki.

"Hi, Kiki," Emme said. "We were just revising for a maths quiz today."

"Good luck," Kiki said, sitting down next to Jesse.

"Do you remember how to do these problems from last year?" Jesse asked Kiki, pointing to his maths book. Then he slapped his forehead. "Of course you do – look who I'm talking to. I am jealous of your brain right now because I am about to F-A-I-L this quiz."

"Well, at least you can spell it," Kiki quipped.

"You are not going to fail!" Emme said, somewhat too cheerily.

Kiki gave her a bad look. She felt kind of territorial when it came to Jesse being friends with other girls. She couldn't help it.

The bell rang and they all gathered up their bags and papers.

Emme's besties came down the aisle to grab their friend. Emme squeezed out of the row to go with them, calling, "See you later, Jesse!"

"Okay, what was *that* about?" Kiki whispered.

"What?" Jesse asked. "What was *what* about?"

"Emme Remmers. And you!"

"What's the big deal? I do have other friends, you know," he replied, stuffing his books into his bag.

"Yeah, and they seem to all be girls!"

"What can I say? The ladies love me." Jesse winked. "Besides, Emme is actually pretty nice. You are totally overreacting."

"Yeah," Kiki said. She took a breath. "I'm sorry to be weird."

"Well, luckily I'm used to your weirdness," Jesse said as they got up and walked to class. "Hey, how did the Supernovas audition go last night?"

"It wasn't an audition!" Kiki made a face. "I'm already in the group, Jesse. But I'm not sure I'll be much help at the competition."

"Oh," said Jesse, chuckling. "So you're only super-human in *our* classes? Not in GCSE-level chemistry? What a shocker. Why are you so hard on yourself?"

Kiki smiled and shrugged and hurried off to her lesson. Jesse always helped put things in perspective. And of course, he made her laugh at the same time.

The hours dragged by all day. Kiki found herself staring at the clock in every lesson.

It was unlike Kiki to be so distracted. Was it the arrival of Auntie Pat? Was it *FTS* she was worrying about? She found herself daydreaming about gooey fudge cake, the same kind she'd tried at Daisy's Desserts. And she thought about how nice it had been that Daisy took time away from bakery work to talk to Kiki the other day.

In social studies Kiki sat near the window overlooking the main street. She watched traffic roar by, including a bus that passed with an enormous billboard advertisement on its side that read *BAKERY BARN COMING SOON*, with fake pictures of a cow and a chicken in chef hats making cupcakes.

There it was again. *Coincidence.* Was this getting weird?

"Kiki? Would you tell us the answer please? What was the first written code of laws?" the teacher boomed.

Kiki quickly looked up and, even though she had *not* been paying very close attention, she scanned her brain and said, "Hammurabi's Code."

"Correct."

Kiki breathed a sigh of relief. Science wasn't her only A+ in the works.

At the end of the day, as Kiki knew Mum and Dad wouldn't be home until later and as Shawn had rugby practice again, Kiki asked Jesse if he wanted to go to Daisy's. She couldn't explain why she wanted to go back there, she just knew she did.

Jesse complied, of course. Chocolate was involved! Well, that and football was cancelled that afternoon.

"How'd you do on the maths test?" Kiki asked as they passed shops and the corner newsstand.

"You mean the quiz?" Jesse replied, spinning the wheels of his skateboard as he carried it.

Kiki nodded. "What's the dif?"

"Quizzes count for less. Which is good for me because I totally tanked it. I knew I would. I think you need to start tutoring me. Or maybe I should ask Emme Remmers?"

"Very funny!" Kiki punched him. "Except that it's *not* funny."

"Kind of is," Jesse teased.

The bakery was bopping on that Friday afternoon. As they approached, Kiki's pulse quickened. It was that crazy, imaginary force field again, some electric power that she felt pulsing inside of her the minute she walked in.

"Hey, Daisy!" Kiki said when she saw the dear, frizzy redhead in charge.

Daisy was busy, but she looked up, flashed Kiki a wide grin and waved.

"Let's grab a table," said Jesse, and he tossed his backpack onto an empty chair.

"What'll it be, my chickadees?" asked the baker called Babs, with her silver hair in a perfect coif and her long nails painted the same shade of silver.

"What's the special today?" Kiki asked.

"Everything! But for today only we have a honey pound cake drizzled with a molasses glaze."

"No way!" Kiki cried. "Honey and molasses? Those are my turtles' names!"

"What are the odds? That's got to mean something cosmic," Babs exclaimed. "So shall I bring two turtle cakes and two forks, then?"

"Just one turtle, please," Jesse said. "What I really want is one of those giant snickerdoodle cookies I saw in the window display that had my name on it."

As Babs laughed and bopped away to get their order, Jesse muttered to Kiki, "Forget turtles. I could eat a horse. I'm starved."

"Yuck!" Kiki cried, and she thought again of the cow and chicken she'd seen advertising Bakery Barn on the bus.

Suddenly loud voices were heard coming from the kitchen. A hush went over the entire place to hear what the ruckus was about. It was Carlos, the male baker Daisy had introduced. He sounded very upset.

"I saw a preview of the new Bakery Barn menu. It has our specialities – including apple bars!

It's not possible! They want to run us out of the neighbourhood!"

"Shhh! Shhh!" someone tried to calm him.

People in the main part of the bakery awkwardly continued to eat their cakes and pastries while they eavesdropped. Daisy rushed into the back to investigate.

"What's going on?" Jesse wondered aloud.

Kiki wasn't sure why there was so much commotion, but she had a hunch. They were talking about the arrival of Bakery Barn, which was being advertised absolutely *everywhere*, as she herself had seen. Did Carlos really think the new place would *steal* Daisy's recipes?

In her excitement for the arrival of as many sweet treats as possible, Kiki neglected to consider the fact that, at the end of the day, a bakery superstore like Bakery Barn would not be a very good thing for Daisy Duncan and her amazing little Daisy's Desserts.

Not at all.

And Kiki began to wonder if maybe there was something she could do to fix that. There was just one problem: She'd be going against her own father.

Chapter 4

Let the bakery wars begin

"I can't believe you both made it home for pizza tonight," Kiki said as she passed the parmesan cheese shaker to Dad.

"Give me some of those red pepper flakes too," Dad said, licking his lips.

"I think I aced my science test today," Kiki said. "And I got back an English essay from last week. A+!"

Dad looked up from his pizza. "I am so proud of you, Kiki. Your mother told me that the Supernovas asked you to participate in a special competition?"

Kiki nodded. "It's the *FTS* science programme.

You've seen that on cable TV, right? I don't really know if I can help them get any of the answers, but I'll try."

"Give them your best, and that's all they can ask for," Dad said.

"And how was your day, sweetheart?" Mum asked, touching Dad's wrist across the table.

"Busy!" Dad said. "I've been working on that new account for the developer of Chef Atrium in the city centre."

Kiki's ears perked up. "What's the deal with that place anyway?"

"It will be a huge, one-stop food shopping and dining experience with a Bakery Barn and other food speciality shops. Everything you could ever need under one roof. And I'm in charge of the publicity," Dad explained. "Which means that I'm responsible for getting people in the door. Have you seen any of our advertisements?"

Kiki bit her lip and nodded. "Everywhere. I even saw one on a bus with a chicken and a cow on it."

Dad didn't seem to notice Kiki's lack of enthusiasm. He just smiled and gave a thumbs up. "Good, then it's working! We have to get the word out. We need to get customers from all over the city. Especially for Bakery Barn. That will occupy an entire floor. Can you imagine?"

"An entire floor ... of that mega building?" Kiki squeaked. "And what's up with the cow?"

"People just seem to love cows," Dad said with a helpless shrug. "And who can resist 900 square metres of cupcakes?"

"That is a lot of cupcakes," Mum agreed, getting up to go into the kitchen.

"There is nothing like Bakery Barn anywhere," Dad insisted, putting on his salesman voice.

Did you ever think that maybe there's nothing like it for a reason? Kiki wanted to say. If there were 900 square metres of bargain cupcakes, would people still want to go to Daisy's tiny neighbourhood bakery?

"What about other bakeries?" Kiki asked quietly.

"What about other bakeries?" Dad asked. "Bakery Barn will beat them all."

Kiki gulped. This was terrible news. Did Dad's company want places like Daisy's Desserts to go out of business? Beat them *all*? It sounded like an attack! Was this the beginning of some kind of bakery war?

"Honey," Dad called out to Mum. "Do we have any dressing for the salad?" He scooped a pile of lettuce and tomato onto the side of his plate.

"I think there's a little Italian left," Mum said, bringing it over and kissing his head. "You said you'd do the dishes, right? I'm wiped out."

Dad nodded. "Go and relax. I'll clean up."

Kiki poked at her slice.

"What's up, K? You're hardly eating your pizza," Dad said, stealing a crust off her plate. "Usually you'd battle me for the last slice."

"Yeah, well not everything has to be a battle, does it Dad?"

"What's *that* supposed to mean?" Dad asked,

pulling back with a confused look. "Someone lost their fighting spirit? Maybe you need some of my favourite red pepper flakes?"

Kiki moped. "You can have the last piece. I lost my appetite."

"What, our first dinner together in days, and this is how it goes?" Dad said.

Kiki didn't mean to totally deflate at the dinner table, but she couldn't stop thinking about poor Daisy. How could any small bakery possibly survive the arrival of a place like Bakery Barn? Was there some formula Kiki could find to stop all this from happening?

But as she tried to fall asleep that night, Kiki couldn't stop thinking about Dad and this job. Maybe she should have paid more attention before now? She had no idea what he really did for work, did she? Could her very own father be the big bully that would bring down a little bakery?

On Saturday mornings Kiki usually slept in, curled deep under the three quilts on her bed next to her stuffed bear, Copper. (Copper had been Kiki's favourite periodic element at the age of five when she'd got him.) But today, she could hardly sleep at all.

Someone knocked on her door. "Hey, sis," Shawn called.

"Go away!" Kiki groaned. "I'm sleeping!"

Shawn ignored her and came in anyway. He sat on the edge of the bed. "Did you see all those papers Dad left on the table last night?" he asked.

"What papers?"

"I saw these advertising scripts, a whole stack of them, about his new work project," Shawn said. "I heard him talking about that other bakery too, the one we were at the other night."

"Daisy's?" Kiki said, sitting straight up in bed. "What about it?"

"Nothing really, just that he had a copy of the menu from Daisy's bakery *right there*."

"What?" Kiki was stunned. She thought back to what she'd heard Carlos say from the back of the bakery. *"They have our apple bar recipe!"*

Maybe Bakery Barn really *was* stealing ideas from Daisy's.

Kiki had seen this before. There were loads of films and TV series about the plight of the underdog. Some tiny shop went up against the chain store. Some poor little restaurant was steamrolled by a big tacky restaurant franchise. The ending was always the same: The underdog fought back and won. But did that only happen in films?

Kiki made up her mind to help Daisy out. The underdog bakery would have to win!

"Maybe we're making more out of this than we need to?" Shawn said. "But I just feel like that place, that Daisy's Desserts, there was something about it that was so ..."

"Magical?" Kiki said.

Shawn nodded. "And I don't even believe in that stuff. But when I saw what Dad was doing, I had to tell you. I don't even know why. I usually don't even talk to you before noon."

"We have a mission," Kiki said, "if we choose to accept it."

Shawn laughed. That was the opening line from every *Mission Impossible* film ever. Those were his favourite films, and Kiki knew it.

They made a plan to show up at the Grand Opening of Bakery Barn, which was scheduled for the next day. They'd see the enemy for themselves and then stage their offensive strategy.

Kiki wasn't sure what the attack would be, or what weapons would be used, but she did know one thing: She would find a way to speak up for Daisy's Desserts. No Bakery Barn was going to get in the way of Daisy's magic.

No way.

That afternoon, Kiki was holed up in her room studying for the *FTS* competition. Mum had driven out to the airport to pick up Auntie Pat. Shawn was at a friend's.

That left Dad, who was in the living room working when Kiki came out for a snack.

"Hey," he said, packing up his briefcase. "I need to step out for a meeting."

"On a Saturday?" Kiki asked.

"Yep, no time to waste. The Grand Opening is tomorrow. I'll be back in an hour or two, okay?"

"Can I come with you?" Kiki asked, suddenly deciding to fast forward her spy plan.

Dad thought for a moment. "I suppose so. You'd have to sit quietly though. Do you have some homework or a book you can read while I have my meeting? They have a huge lobby with TVs everywhere."

"TVs?" Kiki laughed. "Showing what?"

"Cooking programmes, of course."

Kiki nodded. This was too good to be true. It would be even better than the Grand Opening. She could see from the inside what was going on before it even opened. Maybe she could even eavesdrop on Dad's meeting? Kiki's mind raced. She could be like Harriet the Spy in action.

As it turned out, she didn't have to work very

hard to spy. When she and Dad walked into the main part of the new Chef Atrium featuring the 900-square metre Bakery Barn, everything was right there in the open. There was no mystery about signs that read, *Beat the Competition* or *We Offer More Choices than Smaller Bakeries* or *Why Shop Anywhere Else? Free Cupcake with Purchase!*

Dad shook hands with men and women in suits and disappeared into his meeting. Kiki sat on a bench and watched people moving in and out of the shop's entrance. Everyone had on the same apron and wore the same stressed facial expression.

She got up for a glance inside. There were baking supplies and baked goods as far as the eye could see. There were sections divided by flavour or colour. She saw rows of pans and mixers and other baking supplies, decorative toppings, flours and ingredients from around the world and one entire section devoted to colourful fondant, whatever that was. This really was an emporium, not just some run-of-the-mill shop.

But still, there was something missing from this place. No personal touch. No cozy wooden mismatched tables. No hand-letter chalkboard menus. And there was no Daisy.

No magic.

When Dad finally reappeared, Kiki was more than ready to leave. He handed her a pre-wrapped cupcake with a sticker of a barn on top.

"What's this?" she asked.

"A special treat!" Dad said, winking.

"*Hmmm,*" Kiki mumbled.

She turned over the cupcake to see another sticker with the ingredients printed in teeny-tiny type. There were words she recognized from science class like "hydrogenated" and "phosphate" and "diglycerides". There were also some ingredients she'd never heard of before like "locust bean gum".

"Locusts?" Kiki mused aloud. "There are insects in this cupcake?" She made a mental note that she'd have to ask Mr G about that one.

Dad laughed. "This place will have a thousand

flavours of cupcakes," he said, exaggerating as he sometimes did. "No one will be able to resist a place where you can buy and eat just about anything you ever dreamed of. Like Willy Wonka's factory times ten!"

"Do they bake everything here?" Kiki asked, already guessing the answer.

"I think they bake it off-site," Dad replied, seeming distracted as he shuffled through some of his papers.

Kiki nodded and murmured, "Thought so."

The cupcake didn't look anything like the ones Daisy had at her shop. This one was half the size of hers, and it didn't have that fresh-baked, one-of-a-kind, swirly-iced look like the perfectly over-sized, made-with-love ones at Daisy's Desserts.

And Daisy's cupcakes certainly didn't smell like plastic.

"Let's head home," Dad said. "What did you think? I know you were curious. This is an extra-special place, isn't it? "

"I suppose so," said Kiki, even though inside her head she was thinking that this place was extra something all right – extra awful.

Upside-down cake

The Auntie Pat reunion was perfection.

From the moment Mum and Pat got back from the airport, the energy in the Booker flat changed completely. Everyone was so happy to have funny, cheerful Aunt Pat there, and they were relieved that she'd be helping out with their crazy-busy life for a couple of weeks.

After Sunday dinner, the family spent a long time just sitting and talking, catching up on relatives in Jamaica and other news. Pat passed her mobile phone around the table, showing all the new photographs of the cousins and Gammy and Papa back on the island.

Then Aunt Pat wanted to be told about what Shawn and Kiki had been doing in school.

"So I'm in this Supernovas group with– " Kiki started to say.

Shawn piped in. "I was in the group too, last year, Auntie P," he crowed. "It's for Year 10 pupils. I was supposed to stay on as an advisor, but I had to step back because of rugby."

"Wow," Auntie Pat smiled widely. "Wait. You're in what year, Kiki?"

"Seven," Kiki said.

"Kiki is the real deal, Auntie," Shawn said, his brotherly pride coming out. "I hate to admit it, but my sister has some hard-core brains. She knows way more than half my friends in Year 11."

Kiki smiled shyly. Sometimes her brother said the sneakiest nice things.

Auntie Pat clapped her hands together softly. "So what do you do in this Supernovas group? Tell me everything."

"Battle!" Shawn said. "There's a big competition

coming up. It's on TV! They ask all these advanced science questions. Like, describe the difference between Einstein's General Theory of Relativity and his Special Theory of Relativity."

Auntie Pat's eyes got big. "My goodness!" she said. "Kiki, you know the answers to questions like that?"

"Some," Kiki said modestly. She was secretly tempted to answer the actual question about relativity to prove that she did but decided Auntie Pat didn't need to hear some long scientific lecture. Not now. Kiki could hear Jesse's voice in her head: "Don't be such a show off."

"The truth is, Auntie, I'm a back-up, really. It's not a big deal …"

"Yeah, it'll be a *big deal* when you 'back them up' all the way to the championship!" Dad said, reaching over to squeeze Kiki's shoulder.

Everyone laughed. Shawn rolled his eyes like all good brothers do, but Kiki was pretty sure she saw that he was proud too.

The next morning, Kiki got up super-early to squeeze in some study time before the Grand Opening at Bakery Barn. By eleven, Dad was rounding up the troops. Kiki, Shawn and Auntie Pat were all going, while Mum worked a shift at the hospital.

The opening was covered by all the major papers and news stations. The shop got a few local celebrities to appear too, including the woman who chose the daily lottery picks on local news and an assemblywoman dressed up in fancy clothes that actually seemed to match some of the confections. *Dad's idea, of course.* There were TV cameras and balloon animals and a dancing cow and chicken that looked like they'd jumped right off one of the billboard advertisements. Employees were stationed at every entrance, and at the front of every aisle. People crushed together for free cake pops in the same red, yellow and blue colours of the shop's primary logo.

Kiki's dad kept running off to check up on various press, who were scattered around the event.

Auntie Pat, Kiki and Shawn led themselves around the huge shop. It was too much to believe. Kiki had never seen so many baking supplies in one place.

"Where do we even begin?" Auntie Pat said, seeming overwhelmed. The number of boxed cookies and cakes was mind-blowing.

When they'd finally made a few selections, they got in the queue to pay. One of the cashiers put together an enormous box for them to take home and slipped a flyer into their bag.

Kiki grabbed it. Mostly it was a hit list of Bakery Barn's menu. But a few other lines caught her eye. Kiki read them aloud: *"Other bakeries can't compare to the selection at Bakery Barn. Why shop at a small bakery … when you can have the biggest and the best in baked goods? BAKERY BARN beats all other bakeries!"*

She showed it to Shawn and Pat.

"Do you think everyone will go to Bakery Barn now, because of this?" Shawn asked.

"Your father works really hard on this account,"

Auntie Pat said. "You want to support him, no?" She raised her eyebrows at Kiki and Shawn.

Kiki wanted to support Dad, but not if meant destroying Daisy's.

At home, after dinner, Mum remembered the treats the rest of the family had brought home. "Okay, who wants dessert – courtesy of Bakery Barn?" she asked, getting up to make a pot of tea. Pat followed Mum into the kitchen carrying the leftovers while Dad, Shawn and Kiki cleared away the dirty plates and cups.

One thing Kiki didn't mind cleaning up was the flyer from Bakery Barn. She crumpled it up and threw it in the rubbish bin.

Mum ripped open the plastic cupcake wrappers and cut the cakes into quarters so everyone at the table could taste-test more than one kind. Kiki had to admit, they did look pretty impressive. They were a rainbow of colours with different toppings and icing flavours. And Kiki's anger at Bakery Barn faded as her mouth began to water. She reached for an ivory-iced sample, expecting the bright taste of vanilla and toasted coconut. But what she actually tasted was bland and greasy. She grabbed a second piece, dark chocolate with dried cherries on top. Turns out the chocolate icing tasted pretty much the same as the ivory-coloured one. How was that possible? *Blech.*

"*Ooooh*!" Auntie Pat cooed as she grabbed a yellow cupcake. But as she bit into it, she said, "Hmm, I can't tell if it's supposed to be lemon or banana," and she looked at it as if it might offer a clue.

"Nonsense!" Dad cried. "Bakery Barn cakes are supposed to be the best-tasting treats for miles. I'm sure they're still just working out the kinks." And he took a big bite of one with cinnamon crumble on top. "This isn't half bad."

Kiki frowned. "It isn't half good either, Dad. Baked goods are supposed to … well, jump up and hug you!"

"Huh?" Dad looked at her like she was crazy.

"Let's see," Mum interjected, always positive.

"The strawberry seems good, I think. It's just a little too smooth, like maybe too much shortening or something. But it's good, honey. I know Bakery Barn is going to blow the competition out of the water."

Kiki squirmed in her chair.

Shawn had a white and blue cupcake in one hand and a lemon/banana mystery one in the other. "They all just taste sweet to me," he said. But then he looked over at Kiki pointedly. "Not as good as Daisy's, though."

"Daisy's?" Dad asked.

Kiki felt her face get hot. "Just this other bakery. Near school. That's where the Supernovas met the other day."

"Well, Daisy's can't possibly have the selection that Bakery Barn does," Dad said, dismissively. "Pass me one of those marble cupcakes with the sprinkles on top."

After finishing her homework that night, Kiki went online. She found the website for Bakery Barn, which had an enormous page of cupcake photographs with nothing more than the words *COMING SOON* in big red print and the location at the bottom of the page. It was slick and glossy, like a magazine ad. Then she clicked onto the website for Daisy's Desserts.

That home page was much more like a *hug*. It called the stuff inside the shop *Baked Love*. That was exactly what Kiki had been trying to describe to her dad! One of the lines in a blog post caught her eye: *"I think I know exactly what kind of cake I am going to bake for you ... you'll see."* Kiki thought about how Daisy had handed Shawn his favourite treat, right out of the blue. And how she had served Kiki "courage" in the form of cake. There was just a sense of connection that Daisy made with people. A mega store with mega crowds couldn't possibly offer that, could it?

Daisy had posted photographs of each item they baked in their shop. And she showed pictures of the ingredients she used before they became something spectacular. It was like seeing the elements of a science lab before and after the best experiment ever. Everything was natural too. No mention of diglycerides anywhere. Just flour, sugar, butter, eggs ... and love! That wasn't the most scientific of ingredients, but it was just as essential.

For the rest of the night, during her dreams and even upon waking the next morning, Kiki thought of nothing else except the strange predicament of Daisy's bakery. Daisy could hardly fight the big shop that was moving in on her business, could she? For starters, Daisy couldn't brag about 900 square metres. Her shop was only a fraction of that. And she certainly didn't have the budget for big obnoxious bus adverts, not that that was her style, anyway. What could she do to truly compete?

Thankfully, Kiki's bakery obsession waned a little bit once the school week began. From Monday morning right through the week, Kiki was consumed by studying for *FTS*, thinking up and then rejecting ideas for her science recipe assignment and all her other schoolwork. Best of all, Kiki was happily distracted by the arrival of her aunt.

When Kiki got home each afternoon, Pat would check up on her and ask all the right questions: "Did you finish your maths worksheet?" and "Did you proofread that essay?" and "Don't you think you should read an extra chapter in your book just so you're extra prepared?"

And every day she worked out some cool new way to do Kiki's hair. One day she pulled the plaits into a ponytail. The next day she made a thick plait out of the smaller plaits. Pat made life easier. The children could focus more on their schoolwork and activities. And she prepared meals so Mum didn't have to race back from her nursing shifts or classes. And Dad could concentrate on his important clients, especially the one whose Grand Opening had been a major success.

Even though Bradley had told her that she probably wouldn't be needed on the "front line", Kiki kept studying in earnest for the *FTS Show*. She wanted to be ready, just in case, and Auntie Pat's presence made that possible.

So when the Supernovas organized another meet-up at Daisy's Desserts, Kiki invited Auntie Pat to come too, as a thank you. She wanted her to see a bakery that was very different from the mega-bakery her dad was working for. She was also excited to show her teammates how much she'd been studying. She hoped they would be impressed.

Auntie Pat said she'd meet Kiki at the bakery after the Supernovas meeting. They'd try out some of the sweet treats she kept hearing about. Then they could take the bus home together. Time for just the two of them to spend together.

After school, Kiki met up with Jesse, who was also heading to Daisy's to get himself another treat. This time he was planning to get one of her apple bars. As he was working his way through Daisy's list of goodies, one by one, he kept declaring new favourites.

"I just hope it's not too crowded," Jesse said as they walked towards their destination.

"Of course it will be busy! Everyone loves Daisy's!" Kiki said.

But even from a short distance away, Kiki noticed there was no busy buzz at Daisy's bakery as there usually was. In fact, there was only one person sitting at a table with a cup of espresso and a single slice of upside-down cake. *One person*! This was not the hustle and bustle that they were accustomed to seeing at Daisy's after school.

As Kiki walked inside, little bells on the door jingled. The baker named Dina came right over.

"Sit anywhere you can find a spot. We're a little busy ..." Dina said with a smile.

Jesse wrinkled his brow. "Um .... busy?"

"KIDDING!" Dina exclaimed. "I don't know what it is," she said, shaking her head. "We just haven't seen much action this week. Trying to stay positive about the whole deal, but Carlos in the back thinks he knows what's going on. I guess there's a new bakery in town," Dina said in a hushed tone.

"Huh?" Jesse made a face. "What's she talking about?"

"Bakery Barn," Kiki said with a sigh.

Dina gave a tight smile. "That's the one," she said. "It's been all over the news, and we're seeing fewer and fewer customers every day. Here I thought Carlos was being paranoid, but I'm beginning to think he might be right about this conspiracy theory to shut down our little bakery."

"I'm so sorry," Kiki said meekly.

"Stop!" Dina cried. "It's not your fault that we can't compete with the Mega Barn or whatever its name is."

"Bakery Barn," Jesse said.

Kiki felt somehow responsible for all this because of her dad's involvement. She wanted to confess about his public relations work but didn't know what to say, not exactly. So she kept her mouth shut.

Dina beckoned them towards the back. "Come with me," she said. "Come say hi to the team. It'll do them good to see some loyal customers!"

As they stepped into the back area of the shop, Kiki's heart pounded. There was something too-too exciting about the great behind-the-scenes reveal. A few bakers were rushing here and there. The wonderful smell of baking wafted around. There was a thin dusting of flour on *everything*. On the walls were photographs of Daisy's greatest hits, including her "world-famous" apple bars.

Carlos was hard at work, kneading and bopping to music on his headphones. There was a wide spread of ingredients in front of him, but as soon as Dina walked over with Kiki and Shawn, he stopped and brushed the flour off his hands.

"Hello, short friends!" Carlos said jovially, taking off his headphones.

"Kiki and Jesse think you might be right about Bakery Barn," Dina blurted. Then the bell jingled, and she rushed back out front, hoping for customers.

"You do, eh?" Carlos looked interested. "Well, funny you should say that. I've been working here all day to see what I can do with some of our recipes to make them that much better than what the new bakery is serving. They took so many items from our menu, but they don't taste nearly as special as ours. I think we need to be unified in our mission: beat Bakery Barn."

"They're saying *they'll* beat *you*," Kiki said, feeling guilty. "But they can't possibly beat the cakes and cookies here!"

Kiki wanted to tell Carlos that Bakery Barn's food tasted like cardboard, but then she'd have to admit that she'd been there, like a traitor! She considered confessing to Carlos about "the enemy" and the flyer she'd seen, but she didn't want to upset him more. He might even suspect that *Kiki* was the one leaking information to the cow and chicken and whoever else was running the Bakery Barn.

"Your desserts rule," Jesse added. "I consider myself an expert, so I should know!"

Carlos nodded his head. "Now just convince the rest of the world, will you? Can you believe they don't even bake their stuff on the premises? What's the point? Such a shame!"

For a few minutes Kiki and Jesse watched as Carlos explained how he was experimenting with ingredients in the back. He'd been looking over old recipes for days.

"How do you decide what ingredients to use?" Kiki asked him.

Carlos grinned. "I've got a science degree, you know."

"Really?" Kiki said. "Did you know that Bakery Barn uses locust bean gum in their cupcakes?" That tidbit slipped out, but no one seemed to catch on.

Jesse sighed. "Oh great. Now you've both found a way to turn the conversation to the subject of science."

"And with good reason!" Carlos exclaimed. "*All* of baking is science. The kitchen is the greatest laboratory ever. What do you think I'm doing here?" He went over to the sideboard and pulled out a cluster of ingredients: five or six different kinds of apples, brown and white sugar, and small containers of vanilla and almond extract.

"When I make the apple bars – taken from Daisy's wonderful Nana Belle's recipe – I use the basics, but I play around with different flavours and textures of apples. They cook differently. Sometimes I try no sugar too, which can work well with certain sweeter apples. For the good stuff on top of the apple bar, I use glaze in various flavours, or crushed wafers, or just sugar and butter. I try everything until I get it just right."

"You sound like Mr Galipeau, my science teacher," Kiki said.

"I *wish* Mr Galipeau's lectures were this interesting!" Jesse snorted.

Carlos laughed and handed Jesse two different squares and asked him to taste the difference between the two.

Jesse gobbled them both up and licked his fingers. "I think maybe I need to try a few more before I give you my final answer," he said greedily, making Carlos laugh again.

"You need to know all of your ingredients," Carlos went on. "A lot of salt makes a cookie chewier because it absorbs more water. Bicarbonate of soda is used to neutralize acid in a baked mix. It also makes the cake brown a little bit better. And you should always use butter and not margarine. It makes a difference."

"And because it tastes way better," Jesse said. "Even I know that."

"Do you know why?" Carlos asked. "Because butter melts more quickly and blends into a mix better."

"Not to mention it's not full of chemicals like the fake stuff!" Kiki said.

Carlos nodded. "You two definitely belong in my kitchen! Do you know how to get a truly creamy buttercream?"

"Yeah, you go to the shop and get one of those plastic containers full of it!" Jesse quipped.

"Wrong!" Carlos said and made a buzzer sound. "Well, unless of course you want a mouthful of those chemicals you were talking about." He winked. "I was thinking more about the ingredients we have here."

"Mix together butter and sugar," Kiki said, looking at the ingredients in front of them. "Can you use any old sugar?"

"No," Carlos said. "Icing is better because it's powdered. It'll get creamy faster. And heat the butter 'til it's soft but not liquid. That makes it creamier too."

"Wow, you have all the tricks," Jesse said.

"Just science," Carlos agreed. "I just wish that the science of an upside-down cake could turn the business right-side-up. I'm worried the Bakery Barn may take most of our business. But I will keep experimenting until I come up with the winning formula!"

Kiki smiled because she had been looking for a "formula" to solve this problem too. Daisy burst through the swinging doors and approached the huddle. She was surprised to see everyone together, standing near Carlos's station.

"Having a baking convention are we?" she asked. She had a mysterious twinkle in her eye, as usual. "Kiki, your fellow geniuses are waiting outside. I had a hunch you might be back here."

"Oh!" Kiki said. She'd been so entranced by listening to Carlos that she'd nearly forgotten why she was there.

As they headed back through the double doors, Kiki overheard Daisy whispering to Carlos in a low, frustrated tone. Things at Daisy's Desserts were not as jolly as they'd been before the arrival of the other shop – and Kiki could see that the stress was getting to Daisy.

Kiki had to work out how to be a champ at the *FTS* game show *and* make things better at the bakery.

Chapter 6

Brain freeze and a big idea

Kiki came through the kitchen doors, sat down with the other Supernovas and apologized for being late. They gave her a look like they were impressed that she was allowed "behind the scenes". Kiki just gave a small smile and pulled out the list of practice questions from Tamara.

She needed to focus, but she felt like a doughnut – glazed over from worrying about the bakery problem. The topic of today's review sheet was the galaxy. Bradley said that if they were called supernovas, they had to be spot-on with their astronomy knowledge.

Which constellation contains the star Polaris?

About how many light years will take you across the Milky Way?

On which planet is the largest circular storm in the solar system?

Where would we find the largest volcano in the galaxy, and what is it called?

The sun spot cycle is how long?

Kiki felt a brain freeze coming on. Astronomy was not her strong suit. But after a deep breath, Kiki remembered something Dad always said to her: "There is no *can't* in Kiki!" He was trying to be clever, and Kiki didn't care that it didn't even make any sense. It was still encouraging. She knew if he were sitting in the bakery with her right now, he would be telling Kiki that she could do this.

She looked at the questions more closely. She knew the answers to 3 and 4. That was a relief. But it was only 2 out of 5. She flipped over the page to find all the answers.

Ursa Minor

100,000

Jupiter

Mars; Olympus Mons

11 years

Tamara went over all the answers and then moved onto new categories and random questions in no particular order. She talked about ultraviolet rays and nitrogen and deforestation and DNA strands. She reminded the group that even if they studied all the information in all of their science books, there was still a chance that the "fun" categories would stump them. In other words, study hard but be prepared for *anything*.

Daisy came by the table with a tray of apple bars. Sugar fix!

"Compliments of the house!" Daisy said cheerily.

Kiki looked around the very empty "house".

How could Daisy possibly give away free food when the rest of the bakery was so empty inside? Was she *that* nice? Or that crazy?

Or maybe she just believed in this place. Kiki believed in it too.

The Supernovas meeting concluded after two hours and countless apple bars. Just like before, the crew hustled out of the place, leaving Kiki there. But right on time, Auntie Pat appeared. Kiki introduced her to Daisy.

Daisy and Aunt Pat got to talking about Jamaica. Daisy had visited Kingston once for a baking competition, so she asked about things on the island. Auntie Pat was delighted for any chance to talk about home. She made sure to buy some treats to take home to the Booker house from the bakery.

Babs served them after putting six of the yummiest-looking cupcakes into a small box. Kiki couldn't help but notice they looked brighter and moister than the bunch that had come from Bakery Barn.

While Kiki said her goodbyes and thank yous

to everyone at Daisy's bakery, Babs gave Auntie Pat one of the cupcake samples from a tray by the register.

"Thank you, dearie!" Pat cried out.

She and Daisy shared a big hug. A hug? This place made connections between people. Even without the crowds inside the bakery, it still had a warm hum of positive energy. The *baked love* was really working.

"*Mmmmm,*" Auntie Pat said, licking her lips as they exited the bakery. "These are incredible," she whispered, as if telling a secret. "I can taste butter and sugar and lemon zest and coconut and *wow*. I've never had such a good bit of cake in my life. I may just eat every single one in this box!"

"I know," Kiki said. "Too good, right?"

"Better than those ones yer father had the other night," Auntie Pat said and made a "yuck" face. "And this bakery is so cute. Those ladies, Daisy and Baby."

"Babs!" Kiki corrected with a giggle. "Isn't Daisy's Desserts the best?" Kiki said with a sigh.

"Yes, it is one special place," Auntie Pat agreed. "I'll be happy to pick you up there after school *every day*."

"Deal!" Kiki said. They both laughed at that idea. But at the same time, Auntie Pat's response struck a chord in Kiki. In five minutes her aunt had worked out that Daisy's place was beyond special. So it just didn't seem fair that those other cupcakes were being reported as the best in town when they weren't even close.

Why had all the neighbourhood residents deserted this bakery and moved on to Bakery Barn when Daisy's was so, so, SO much better?

"You've got apple bar crumbs on your shirt, love," Auntie Pat said to Kiki.

Kiki looked down and brushed them off, and suddenly, like a bolt out of the blue, Kiki got a great big, wonderful idea.

She knew *exactly* how she could help Daisy's Desserts get its customers to come back. Kiki had a plan to help win the bakery war. She was going to make sure that everyone stopped *deserting* Daisy's place, and she'd do it without undercutting Dad's bakery. There was room for two bakers in town and Kiki would make sure everyone knew it.

Chapter 7

Don't desert Daisy

As soon they she got home, Kiki sketched her idea onto blank paper. It was a picture that had popped into her mind and sparked the whole idea. A picture of a neon blue T-shirt, a lot like her other clever slogan T-shirts. This one would read: *Don't Desert Daisy's Desserts* in big, funky yellow letters. Kiki's English teacher would be proud of her use of homophones!

On the back of the T-shirt, she had a big, yummy cupcake with the words *100-per cent homemade* stretched over the bottom of it. And best of all, swirled into the top of the cupcake that spilled over the muffin case would be the word "love" in a curly, fancy script. Daisy's cupcakes were baked love, after all.

And then, below the cupcake, she wrote the part that she hoped her dad would like:

> *Buy your supplies*
> *at the other guys'*
> *but eat your sweets*
> *at Daisy's!*

She didn't want to badmouth Bakery Barn, or hurt her dad's work, no matter what the circumstances. Kiki hoped her T-shirts would encourage people to shop at Bakery Barn for their baking needs, but still come to Daisy's for their baked goods. That seemed fair to her.

That night at dinner, Kiki was nervous to tell Dad about her T-shirt idea. She was worried that he would hate it. But he was caught late at a meeting. Mum was at the library cramming for an anatomy test. It was just Auntie Pat, Kiki and Shawn for dinner, so Kiki shared her idea with them. And she decided *not* to tell her dad ... at least not yet.

Kiki showed Shawn and Pat her drawings and explained her plan. Shawn high-fived her. Auntie Pat nodded proudly. They both loved it.

Pat found a website where they could design their own T-shirt with that slogan on it. Kiki had enough in her savings to order ten shirts for two pounds each. Shawn said he'd pay for ten more. And Auntie Pat generously paid the delivery fee. Judging from the sparse crowd they'd seen at Daisy's, there was no time to lose! In just two days, they'd have their T-shirts.

Shawn gave Kiki practice science questions all weekend long, but it was hard to focus when Kiki was thinking so much about ways to get business back for Daisy's bakery.

Kiki could tell that Shawn was distracted too. He totally understood that Daisy's was something special. It was the delicious desserts, the cozy atmosphere, the friendly bakers – all of those things plus more that added up to something magical.

Tuesday, Shawn actually skipped rugby practice to come home after school and meet up with his sister. The package was waiting for them. It came in a white box marked *T-Riffic*!

"It's here!" Shawn shouted. They ripped open the box in the lift on the way up to their flat. The shirts looked *fantastic*.

They each wriggled into one over their clothes and knocked on their front door.

Auntie Pat peered through the peephole at Kiki and Shawn in their T-shirts. "Ta-da!" they both yelled.

The lock clicked, and the door swung open. "Oh, goody! They look marvellous!" Auntie Pat declared.

"This box is real heavy," Shawn said, hoisting it up. "I thought we ordered twenty."

"Well," Auntie Pat confessed. "I couldn't help myself. I ordered three times as many!"

Kiki squealed and threw her arms around Pat.

"You're the best," Kiki shrieked. "I just know this is going to work. And thanks, bro, for helping out."

Shawn shrugged. "Anytime, sis. It's for a good cause."

They threw a load of shirts into a duffel bag and headed over to Daisy's. If they were excited, Kiki could only imagine how excited Daisy, Babs, Dina and Carlos would be.

The bakery was quiet again, just like it had been the week before. With the big new Bakery Barn competing for business, it seemed as if many people had forgotten all about Daisy's. There were only a couple of tables with people at them. At least the ones who were seated there looked like satisfied customers, with big pastries and even bigger smiles on their faces. Kiki could see that Daisy's magic was as powerful as ever.

Kiki found Babs straightening a glass case filled with miniature pies. She was all dolled up with film-star eyelashes and a bouffant. Her face lit up when the three walked in, but Kiki could tell she was putting on a brave front for them.

"Well, hello," Babs said. "If it isn't the science whizz kids!"

Kiki smiled. "And you remember our Auntie Pat. Can we talk to you for a minute?"

Babs closed the glass case and came around the counter. Kiki looked at Shawn and then in unison they slipped off their jackets to reveal their T-shirts and spun to show Babs both sides. Then Kiki handed a shirt to Babs.

"I know it's not fancy and you're always dressed up but ..."

"THIS IS THE BEST THING I'VE EVER SEEN!" Babs yelped. "AND I'VE SEEN A LOT!"

Daisy came running from the kitchen. "What on Earth?" She saw Kiki and Shawn, and then she saw their shirts. She looked confused. Then a broad smile stretched across Daisy's face.

And in that moment, Daisy Duncan began to glow, literally to *shine* like a firefly, like a log lit up at the bottom of a stone fireplace. A sunny warmth spread over her.

"Did you make these?" Daisy blubbered.

Kiki tugged on Auntie Pat. "We did it together," Kiki said. "And my brother Shawn too."

Babs was all giggles. She yanked her T-shirt right over her apron. Then she raced into the back to give one to Carlos.

Daisy couldn't stop staring, her hand on her mouth, radiating her glow.

"I think your love for this place has changed everything," Daisy finally said. "What do we want to do with these shirts?"

"We could sell these right here in the bakery!" Carlos declared as he marched out of the kitchen clapping his hands together. "These are brilliant! Leave it to the brainiac kids to come up with these!"

Kiki laughed. "Thanks, Carlos."

"I mean it!" Carlos went on. "I've been saying this since I first caught wind of *that other place.* We can't take this sitting down. We are at war with Bakery Barn, and that's all there is to it. We need to fight for our customers!"

A table of senior citizens – the only people in the bakery – raised their fists in the air and shouted, "We're with you!"

One of them stood up and said, "I'll take one. How much?"

"You want a T-shirt?" Kiki asked. She tugged on the one she was wearing. "This T-shirt?"

The old woman nodded. "You're too cute."

Auntie Pat whispered into Kiki's ear. "Charge her five pounds. We can keep two to pay ourselves back, and the extra three can go to Daisy to help advertise."

"Five pounds!" Kiki pronounced to the woman, who was already pulling out her wallet.

"That's a total bargain. And for such a worthy cause! You should make T-shirts for kids too," the woman said. "I know some of my neighbours would definitely fight for this place. We all come here. This city is too fickle, always distracted by the shiny new thing dangled in front of them."

"Thank you for saying that," Daisy said.

Kiki could see Daisy beginning to blush. Her skin went all pink and hot. She fanned herself and gave the old woman a hug.

"See?" Carlos threw his arms into the air and grabbed Babs around the waist.

Babs smoothed down her 'do and grinned. "Bringing back the happy!"

Daisy looked squarely at Kiki. "I can't believe this. I can't believe you did this for us!"

"She had a vision," Auntie Pat explained. "It all came from her. And then we just ran with it!"

Shawn was strutting around, showing off his rugby muscles and yelling, "Fight for Daisy's!" Carlos gave him a high-five and started flexing his own muscles.

And so it went. They sold four more shirts right then and there, and then a woman came in with a buggy and bought two more. Daisy got shirts for everyone who worked there too. Kiki felt like King

Midas, turning everything she touched into gold. Or in this case, pounds for Daisy's.

And the T-shirts were only the beginning.

The power of Daisy's Desserts was about to work its true magic.

A recipe for friendship

Of course Jesse laughed when he saw Kiki's T-shirts.

"You just decided to make these?" he chuckled.

"Are you making fun of me for doing this?" Kiki grunted. "I can't believe you would– "

"Making *fun*?" Jesse exclaimed. "Are you kidding? These are the most amazing things I've ever seen. You came up with this idea to save the world while the rest of us were zoning out playing video games? Impressive!" He bowed in front of Kiki. "I'm not worthy," he crowed.

"Daisy's first – the world next," Kiki said with a laugh.

She got permission from the school principal to sell the shirts at lunch. And Daisy had provided samples of goodies to give away with the shirts. Auntie Pat had already placed a reorder. She got some in other colours too – pink, green and white.

Mr Galipeau marched up to the table where the T-shirts were on display and threw down a £10 note.

"I'll take one," he said. "Keep the change."

Kiki mouth gaped open. "Thanks, Mr G!"

"Just do a good job at that *FTS Show*, okay? The Supernovas are counting on you and so am I."

Kiki saluted. "Gotcha, Mr G. I'll do my best."

Before he walked away, he grabbed a mini-sample of apple bar and immediately gave it a thumbs up.

Everyone wanted a T-shirt. They also wanted as many samples as they could shove into their mouths. And after tasting the treats and hearing about Daisy's, they definitely wanted it to stay in business.

When Emme Remmers strolled by with her friends, Jesse straightened up like he wanted to be on his best behaviour for her. Kiki just laughed and slugged Jesse's shoulder. He was acting so obvious!

"This is so amazing," Emme told Kiki.

Kiki shrugged. "Yeah, thanks."

"Seriously," Emme continued. "When I was having some issues with my parents earlier this year, I spent a lot of time at Daisy's place. She helped me make these spun sugar cookies for my parents' anniversary."

"She helped you bake?" Kiki asked. "I've heard spun sugar is really hard to do!"

"Well, I'm not really very good," Emme said, twirling her hair with one finger. She pushed her cat's eye glasses back up onto her nose. "I mean, I'm not *terrible*, but ..."

"Daisy's super nice, isn't she?" Kiki said. "Magical, even!"

"Yes, she really is!" Emme and Kiki smiled at each other, so glad that someone else felt the same way. One of the hall bells rang, and Emme had to run. "See you around!"

Jesse just stood there smiling.

"You didn't even say hi to her!" Kiki chastised.

"What? I thought I was supposed to ignore her. That's what you told me to do."

"I never said those exact words. You lie."

Jesse giggled. "You're hilarious, Keeks. Hold on – another lunch crowd is moving in now."

"We only have like ten left. My aunt is going to have to order more. This is incredible."

A group of boys came and gave Jesse fist bumps. While they were all talking, a girl called Maggie with red curly hair came over to the table.

"That's pretty cool," the girl said. "I know Daisy's Desserts. She made everything so much better for me."

"You know Daisy too?" Kiki asked, amazed. "From the bakery?"

Maggie nodded. "*Don't Desert Daisy's Desserts* is so clever. Did you think that up?"

They talked for a few minutes about sugar-related topics and their Daisy connection. Maggie said her grandmother might even be able to make a donation for Daisy's cause.

"Wow," Kiki said. "That would be great!"

A final end-of-lunch bell rang, and the deputy head came around to make sure Kiki and Jesse moved all of their stuff and swept the floor clean.

"So many people know Daisy already," Kiki said, bursting with excitement.

Jesse pointed to her shirt. "And now they won't *desert* her."

Kiki moaned. "Yeah, Jesse, I get it. I made it up, remember?"

As he headed to his class, Jesse called out, "Hey, good luck tomorrow!"

"Thanks!" Kiki said, remembering with a shock that *tomorrow* was the *FTS Show*! She couldn't believe it had come so quickly. It seemed like the Supernovas had only just asked her to participate. And now, here it was. So much had happened since then!

After school, Kiki boarded the usual bus and headed home, past the usual supermarket, dry cleaners, florist shops and then – there it was – bright, open, with gleaming silver doors and a huge sign out front: Bakery Barn. It looked like there were a lot of people going in and out. The bus stopped to unload passengers.

Kiki could see from her seat on the bus that the shop windows were packed with all kinds of creative displays. There were cupcake towers and one enormous wedding cake with a bride and groom mannequin standing nearby. There were words on the window glass in front of them: *Baked with Love.*

Kiki nearly stood right up in her seat. "You can't write that!" she cried. That was Daisy's slogan!

"Have a seat young lady," a woman with a strange accent said.

"I just– " Kiki was huffing and puffing now. "That bakery is stealing ideas!"

"I can't eat sweets," the woman said curtly. "Bakeries don't mean much to me."

"I agree with you," a man said to Kiki from the row of seats behind her. "Have you been inside that place? All show and no substance."

Kiki nodded. "Exactly!" she said. Then she sat back down again and looked out as the bus pulled away.

Auntie Pat was home cooking some kind of great-smelling jerk chicken dish when Kiki walked into the flat. She stopped to hug Pat and tell her about their amazing success at the T-shirt sale. Then, after a quick hello to her turtles, she went into her bedroom and pulled out her binder with all the science worksheets and study lists.

Mr Galipeau had given her a few targeted study sheets to help her revise for the programme. There was one on human anatomy. (Kiki was sure she'd memorized all the body parts and she had even helped test her mum for her nursing test.) There were three different sheets describing the elements. Kiki carefully looked over the periodic table again to make sure she could recall all the symbols. Iron was Fe. Helium was He. She was okay with the easy ones. But she had trouble with the weirder ones, like Cn for Copernicium. She couldn't remember what that even was. Something else to study!

"I counted the money," Auntie Pat said, bounding into the room. "We have sold nearly fifty T-shirts already! I just ordered fifty more! Daisy offered to pay for the shirts, but I told her we'd handle it. My stars, I feel like we're doing something useful."

Kiki jumped up and threw her arms around Pat. "Thanks for filling in the blanks," she said to her aunt. "That's what Mum always says, but it's true. It's so much nicer to have you in this with us and to get excited about it too."

"I can tell, Kiki," Auntie Pat said. "You're going to change the world."

"I'm not solving world problems, Auntie," Kiki said. "We're talking about cupcakes, here."

"Well," Auntie Pat said, "That bakery is Daisy's

world, and you're saving that. And you've got such creative ideas."

"I'm a scientist," Kiki said modestly. "Not creative. Not really."

"Science is creative," Pat said. "You see the world and all of its moving parts. That takes a huge brain *and* imagination. There's so much to take in."

Kiki had never thought about science in exactly that way. It made it sound so much more ... *personal*. All these facts meant more to Kiki than just numbered items on a study sheet. She cared about weather, animals, space, technology and food – all of it!

When Auntie Pat went back to the kitchen, Kiki powered up her desktop computer. She plugged in DAISY'S DESSERTS. She clicked on a blog post that Daisy had written just yesterday.

Hello, Sweeties!

How is everyone? I've been baking like mad with my right hand man, Carlos. We have been developing some exotic new recipes with mango cream and more coconut. You asked for it! We also are planning a big concert evening to bring out the neighbourhood sweet teeth.

Have any of you had a chance to visit the new bakery up First Avenue? I hear it is a lovely – if ginormous – shop with every possible spatula and cookie sheet you could ever wish to purchase. But it also sells baked goods. I encourage you to try it out! Let me know what you think. There's no reason why two bakeries can't co-exist in perfect harmony ...

Kiki stopped after reading that. How could Daisy say those things without being angry? She'd had all her best recipes ripped off by the mega bakery. Daisy had every right to scream at those people, not be nice to them. But she took the more courageous route. Like always.

That just fuelled Kiki even more to keep fighting for Daisy.

Chapter 9

A delicious piece of pi

The day of the *FTS Show* finally arrived. With rain. It was being held early on Saturday morning. Kiki was prepared for pretty much anything – except lousy weather. And now here was the rain, pouring. What luck!

Kiki had planned on wearing heels and a pretty dress under her coloured lab coat. But now the weather was threatening with its heavy grey clouds and hint of electricity in the air. Why wear a dress when nobody would see it beneath the lab coat, anyway?

Kiki already had her raincoat on when Mum came in with a cup of coffee. One of the best gifts

Auntie Pat brought with her was coffee from the Blue Mountains of Jamaica, the real taste of home for Mum.

"Dad and Shawn just left for Shawn's rugby tournament. Hope he does well as it's his final one. But I know they're so disappointed to miss the *FTS Show*," Mum said. "Anything you need before we go?"

"What else could there be?" Kiki blurted out nervously.

"Oh, Kiki. You're shaking," Mum said as she smoothed Kiki's plaits into neat bundles and pulled them back with ribbon. "You look so grown up all of a sudden." She kissed Kiki's forehead.

"Mum, I've looked the same all year."

"Well," Mum said, choking back some kind of frog in her throat. "I think you look especially grown up today."

Kiki's stomach was all butterflies. "I'm nervous, Mum. I'm only in Year 7. Everyone else is so much cleverer."

"Shhhh! That's not true. You are just as clever as anyone there. And nobody has all the answers."

"I'm just not sure I can do this." Kiki's voice came out in a whisper.

"Are you worried about the science programme or something else?" Mum asked. "Are you worried because your dad still doesn't know about the T-shirts?"

Kiki bit her lip. "He'll see the T-shirts soon enough. It's going to be all over."

"Well, Dad will be impressed by the word play on the T-shirts, that's for certain. The advertising copywriter in him will *love* that part."

"I had fun with that, but what I really want is to be a famous scientist one day – maybe even a food scientist," Kiki admitted.

"You're already on your way," Mum said. "Maybe for starters you can help Bakery Barn improve their cardboard cupcakes?"

They laughed together.

Mum took Kiki by the shoulders. "Kiki, I think

what you're doing is creative and inspired and brave. Now, let's get out of here before the rain gets worse, okay?"

Kiki grabbed her stack of science study sheets. She realized that whatever she didn't already know, she was not going to learn now. But she wanted to cram anyway. It felt like everything had slipped from her mind, like she knew *nothing*.

Kiki, Mum and Auntie Pat grabbed a taxi and headed to the studio where the programme was recorded. Inside, tables were set up for contestants and chairs for audience members. There were cameras on both sides of the room too, to capture every nervous tic, apparently. Kiki's nerves were nearing panic mode. She didn't want to be filmed today. What if she said something totally dumb and then saw her wrong answer turned into some kind of viral rap video on the Internet?

Courage, Kiki said to herself.

A producer checked Kiki in and traded her raincoat for a purple lab coat.

"Hey there, Brainiac Junior!" a voice said from behind Kiki. It was Tamara, looking as cool as ever with her short spiky hair dyed purple today. Everything about Tamara seemed effortless, but Bradley and Sam looked nearly as nervous as Kiki. She took some comfort in realizing that she was not the only one.

The directors of the event asked participants to check into the judging table as a team.

Kiki's pulse raced. Thank goodness she'd followed Mum's advice and loaded up with extra deodorant. She considered hiding under her chair until the whole thing was over. Then she caught a glimpse out of the corner of one eye: Jesse and Emme were sitting near Mum and Auntie Pat. Jesse held up a big sign that said: *Supernovas: So Bright, You're Gonna Need Shades.* Good ol' Jesse.

"Remember," Sam told her as they were about to begin. "You probably won't have to say anything. No one will call on you ... unless there's this tricky thing that happens where we lose a point and the other team gets to choose which player has to respond to a three-part sudden death question. Then you might get picked. But the chances of that happening are super slim."

Kiki nodded. She hoped he was right. She could stand still and participate silently. No problem.

The emcee was a lecturer from a city university. She must have been six feet tall. She seemed that big anyway. Her brain was probably big too. Kiki was pretty sure that the brains inside this room could solve world problems. Her nervous Year 7 self was trembling.

"Shall we begin?" the emcee boomed.

Paired teams met up for each round of competition. The purple team, aka the Supernovas, aka *their* team, got to watch a few rounds before they had to compete. That was good because then they had a chance to get a feel for the questions and the level of difficulty.

When the Supernovas were called up for the first time, Kiki held her breath. The lights glared, and the cameras were trained on them like hawks. Kiki probably would have passed out if Bradley hadn't nudged her and reminded her to breathe.

The first question was read aloud.

"What is the approximate distance in light years across the Milky Way?"

They were ready for that one. It had been on Tamara's list when they met at Daisy's. Of course it was Bradley who hit the buzzer and called out his answer, "100,000."

The panel of judges said, "CORRECT."

The foursome high-fived around their circle.

Tamara whispered, "We can do this!"

Kiki wanted to be enthusiastic too, but everything was moving so quickly. It was already time for question two.

"These are the building blocks of polymers."

"Monomers!" Sam called out after buzzing in.

Kiki knew that answer, but it would have taken her a minute to think of it under all this pressure. She gulped. What else could they possibly ask for a stumper?

"For what is

$C6H12O6+6O2 \rightarrow 6CO2+6H2O+energy$

the balanced chemical equation?"

Since this science question was numeric, an image of the question appeared on a screen simultaneously. Kiki's head was spinning. This was more advanced science than she was used to. But Tamara didn't need the visual aid or any extra time either. She buzzed right in.

"Cellular respiration," she said coolly.

After several more questions, a bell rang. The Supernovas had answered the most questions correctly and would be heading to the next round. Their opponents, the Lunar Rovers, came up empty.

Kiki breathed a sigh of relief. She hadn't had to answer any, as Sam had predicted. The quiz show action continued much in the same way for another hour. Then it was narrowed down to semi-finalists and then the final two teams: Purple and Red. It would be a Supernovas vs Nanotechs in the final round. Kiki had not yet answered a single question on her own in all those rounds of play, but she was relieved to discover she had at least known several of the answers.

And then that "super slim" chance happened, and the other team had the opportunity to pick one member of the purple team to answer a trio of questions.

"Don't worry," Tamara promised. "You don't know that they'll ask *you* to answer."

Kiki shook her head. The other team was *totally* going to choose Kiki to answer. They had seen that she hadn't answered a single question all day, so they would know she was the weakest link. She was doomed.

The emcee shuffled some envelopes and conferred with the other judges. They asked the red team who would be their choice to answer the questions.

"The girl on the end."

Kiki. Of course.

Kiki's ears were ringing. She heard her name and then everything went blank.

"It will be okay," Bradley whispered.

"We're done," Sam groaned.

"Shut up!" Tamara whispered. "Kiki, you'll be great."

Kiki was running over those science sheets in her head again. She had to stay focused.

"Ms Booker," the emcee said. "Your category is Food Chemistry."

Kiki's nose twitched. Maybe *this* was what the universe had been trying to tell her all along. She couldn't believe that of all the topics in all the science books in all the world, she was about to get questions about ... *baking*?

"Are you ready?" the emcee asked.

Kiki let out a long breath and nodded. "Ready spaghetti."

Everyone smirked. She hadn't meant to use an expression from when she was a child, but it slipped out. *How to sound like a Year 7 pupil!* she scolded herself.

"Your first question is: Sodium bicarbonate is commonly used as what?"

Kiki clamped down on the buzzer. "Bicarbonate of soda!" she cried.

Tamara, Bradley and Sam all cheered.

"Question number two: What is the Maillard Reaction?"

Kiki wanted to scream. She knew the answer to this one too!

"The Maillard reaction is the browning and deepening of flavours caused by the reaction between an amino acid and a reducing sugar."

"*No way.* I didn't even know that," Bradley murmured in awe.

Kiki took a sip of water. Tamara put her hand on Kiki's arm. "You've got this."

The emcee looked at the card in front of her and then leaned in to confer with the judges. "Correct!" she boomed. "The third question is a riddle."

A riddle? Kiki thought. She wanted to raise up her hand and politely request a recess, like she was in a courtroom. She needed more time to think. How do you prepare for a riddle?

"Listen closely before answering," the emcee continued. "This autumn treat might have been inspired by both Archimedes and Sir Isaac Newton."

The room fell silent.

"Tell us the name of the treat in letters and numbers and why those scientists are connected to it."

Kiki felt a bead of sweat slither down her back. Tamara looked upset. Kiki saw her out of the corner of her eye, biting her lip nervously. Bradley had a blank stare. Sam covered his face.

"Take your time," the emcee said.

The spotlights burned, the cameras stared and

the room was silent. Kiki imagined herself at the dinner table with Shawn, reading from their favourite brain teaser book. That's all this was – with a little scientific knowledge thrown in for good measure.

"Well," Kiki started to respond. She took another deep breath. *Courage*. "The answer is ... apple pie."

Everyone in the room gasped.

"Can you please elaborate, Ms Booker?"

"I think it comes from the legend of Newton watching an apple fall from a tree, which led him to develop the theory of gravity. And Archimedes calculated the value of pi, which rounds to 3.14159265359. Which gives you apple *pi*". Kiki made air quotes for "pi".

The emcee smiled. "Absolutely, one-hundred per cent right, Ms Booker. And with that answer, your team takes first place in the competition!"

Applause broke out, and in that moment, Kiki felt everything in slow motion. She saw Mum and Auntie Pat howling and clapping in one corner of the room. She'd been so focused she hadn't even registered their hoots and yells throughout the match.

"Congratulations!" the emcee came over to shake Kiki's hand. "I understand you are a Year 7 pupil, which makes your victory even more impressive. Well done!"

"I can't believe you got it right!" Sam said.

"I can," Bradley said. "Shawn would be proud. I'm glad he asked you to join Supernovas. He was right. You're one clever girl."

Tamara threw her arms around Kiki. "My sister in science!" she screeched. "You rocked!"

"I knew you before you were famous, Kiki Booker!" Jesse shouted, coming up and waving his poster. Emme appeared behind him and added, "You were amazing!"

Kiki smiled and gave Jesse a subtle wink.

Suddenly, Kiki was swarmed with people. She realized that this was her chance! Deciding to take advantage of this big moment, Kiki snapped off her purple lab coat to reveal her *Don't Desert Daisy's Desserts* T-shirt, standing up tall so everyone could read it. It must have looked so weird with everyone else all dressed up, but she didn't care. She wanted everyone to read the message, to know about Daisy's predicament.

Cameras flashed wildly. And just like that, Kiki Booker got a firm foothold in the bakery war.

"What's the meaning of your shirt?" someone asked.

Kiki looked at Auntie Pat and Mum, who were both giving her a big thumbs up.

"Well," Kiki explained. "It's something my friends and I are doing because we want to support this really great bakery called Daisy's Desserts. Do you know it? They've got delicious, made-from-scratch desserts, and they are a small business that provides a great service to their neighbourhood."

Everyone in the room was buzzing. People took out their phones so they could snap photos of Kiki's shirt and search for the name of Daisy's bakery. If people hadn't heard of it before, they certainly would now.

Tamara, Sam and Bradley patted Kiki on the back.

"Hey, Kiki," Tamara asked. "Do you have any more shirts?"

Kiki smiled and reached into her bag to pull out *Don't Desert Daisy's Desserts* T-shirts for the whole team.

Kiki looked back at the three of them and felt so relieved. She had not only survived the quiz show ordeal, she'd helped to win it! And now she had a chance to get her message about Daisy's Desserts out to all these people.

When the Supernovas took the stage to accept their award in their matching T-shirts, everyone cheered.

Bradley leaned over and whispered, "This whole thing is genius."

"Kiki really takes the cake!" Tamara cheered.

Chapter 10

One clever cookie

Kiki had no idea that a little quiz show for kids would get so much attention online. When she made the spur-of-the-moment decision to reveal her T-shirt, one of the parents watching took a short video. That was posted online. Then a news reporter saw it. And from there it went crazy.

It was Shawn who discovered all the hype when he logged onto the computer to work on his essay that evening before dinner. He spotted his sister under the "trending" column. Someone had written a short bit about standing up for local businesses and how "one teenager can make a difference".

"I'm not even a teenager yet!" Kiki laughed. "I'm

twelve!"

"You always were advanced for your age," Shawn joked. Then he broke into a huge smile. "Do you realize what a big deal this is? I wish I'd been there to see it!"

Kiki hugged him. "I'm glad you weren't. Otherwise your team wouldn't have won the rugby tournament. *You* had your own best day."

"Thanks, sis," Shawn said. "I missed you, though. But hey, I represented!" He pulled out his phone to show Kiki a selfie of him wearing his Daisy's shirt over his uniform.

"Kiki!" Auntie Pat came into the room with a pad of paper. "Can I have your autograph, please?"

"Oh, Auntie Pat," Kiki said. "I just want people to know about Daisy's Desserts – I don't want them to know *me*!"

"Yeah, too late for that," Shawn said. He clicked on another short article on "Inside Beat", a local gossip site with pictures of celebrities. They'd polled a few about the video from the science fair. One of the celebs wondered aloud what Kiki's name was. Soon another person on a message board posted, "That girl goes to my school. Her name is Kiki Booker."

After that, Kiki's name accompanied the video.

"How does word get around so fast?" Kiki asked.

While she, Auntie Pat and Shawn watched the video, the views went from a meagre 2,068 to 32,745! This thing was going viral fast.

Auntie Pat looked proud but then started shaking her head. "Your dad is going to pitch a fit when he sees all this, you know."

"It's only a matter of time before Bakery Barn works out that Kiki Booker is related to Dad, right?" Shawn said.

"Right," a gruff voice said from the doorway.

It was Dad. Right there. He knew.

"Would you three mind explaining this viral video to me, please?" he asked. He didn't look angry, just curious.

"Um …" Kiki was tongue tied. "Am I in trouble?"

"Trouble?" Dad grinned. "Quite the opposite, my

dear. Let me tell you why."

Dad collapsed onto one of the squishy sofas in the living room and took off his shoes. It had been a long, long day. He'd had a meeting with another client before Shawn's rugby tournament. Then, afterwards, he'd got the call from the manager of Bakery Barn. "I think we have a situation," the manager had said and asked Dad to take a taxi up to the shop straight away.

"While you were at the science competition making yourself famous, something else was going on at the shop," Dad said. "Shawn, do a search for Bakery Barn Protest. See what comes up."

Shawn hit a few keys, and a short video from a mobile phone popped up. There were at least twenty people crowded inside the lobby of the Bakery Barn. And every single one of them was wearing one of Kiki's T-shirts. Kiki recognized the older woman who had bought the very first T-shirt. She was arguing with one of the sales people on the floor. It wasn't an angry confrontation, but the battle lines were clear.

"Don't Desert Daisy!" the crowd of people cheered.

Kiki's stomach did a backflip. Those nerves were acting up again. It had been such a crazy day – and she hadn't even known about *half* the crazy!

"So what happened, Dad?" Shawn asked.

Auntie Pat didn't say much. She stood there with her arms crossed, looking at her brother-in-law for an answer. "Yeah, mon, what happened then?"

Dad smiled. "Luck smiled upon us *all*," Dad said. "You think I'm going to say that the manager of Bakery Barn was upset. And he was, a little, but he was also clever. That's why he hired me, after all!"

"Dad, really?" Kiki moaned.

"No, seriously," Dad continued. "Here's what happened. The manager talked to the angry protestors. He told them that he never wanted to put Daisy's Desserts or any other bakery out of business. In fact, he told the protestors that they'd be scaling back their baked good offerings to better focus on their strengths – baking supplies. Bakery Barn wants to fill the gaps in the marketplace, not take over the marketplace."

"But Dad, you said you wanted to beat them all!" Kiki reminded him.

"Yeah, Dad," Shawn added. "I remember, that is what you said."

"Well ..." Dad said. "I was wrong. There's room for all of these businesses. Whoever came up with that T-shirt idea is brilliant. We know that Bakery Barn isn't ever going to give customers personal attention like Daisy's. But they can offer a thousand different cooking and baking products ... and a pastry or two while they're at it."

Kiki climbed onto the sofa and put her head on Dad's shoulder. "The person who made those T-shirts was me, Dad."

"You?" he looked at Kiki like she had sprouted a second head.

"Well, Shawn and Auntie Pat helped, but it was my idea, so I'm responsible. I'm sorry if I got you into trouble. I just wanted to do something to help out the underdog. You always told us to follow our hearts."

"Yes, I did," Dad said, kissing the top of his daughter's head. "I'm not mad. And neither is Bakery Barn. In fact, I'm proud of you. That's a pretty impressive marketing campaign you pulled off, Kiki. And by now I'm guessing that Daisy's Desserts once again has a parade of customers – and new ones from other parts of the city too. I checked out her blog by the way."

"She's magical, Dad, *really.*"

"Well, she's a clever businesswoman, that's for certain. She already has such a loyal following. And I saw that she used the phrase *Baked Love* everywhere. So I told the Bakery Barn team that we needed to find a new slogan. Just to show good faith."

"You did?" Kiki squealed. She gave Dad a huge kiss on his balding head.

"Okay, okay," Auntie Pat clapped her hands.

"Your mum will be home from the library any minute, and you need to help me get this table set."

"Wait!" Kiki said. She ran into the other room and then back to Dad. "Here!" she said, throwing one of the *Don't Desert Daisy* T-shirts into his lap.

Dad chuckled. "Okay, okay, I'll put it on. But first you have to tell me about *FTS*. What's this I hear about some twelve-year-old saving the day?"

Everyone laughed and headed into the dining room for Auntie Pat's special curried goat.

The next day, Kiki woke up at the crack of dawn. She was restless. All the excitement of the week's activities had her wound up tightly. She curled up on the sofa in front of the TV. Kiki had gone from ordinary girl to science whizz to viral superstar, and her head was spinning. There was no scientific formula for how to handle this, was there? It felt good to be lazy for a change, didn't it? Cartoons helped.

Mum and Dad gave Kiki permission to go to Daisy's Desserts that afternoon, just to check in and say hello. After all, she was a bit of a superstar.

She called Jesse and asked him to meet her there. Jesse said of course he would be there. In fact, he had already sent her a dozen texts about the video, which he claimed to have watched one hundred times.

Jesse was riding his skateboard on the pavement outside of Daisy's when Kiki arrived.

"You would not believe what's going on in there," Jesse said. "Crazy."

"What?" Kiki asked, worried that something had backfired.

Jesse opened the door and gestured towards the dozens of people crammed into the bakery. As Kiki walked in the door, people turned and pointed at her. Daisy rushed over. Then, all at once, everyone began to clap.

"And here she is!" Daisy announced. Kiki wasn't sure how to take all of the attention. So much clapping is like a rainstorm, fast and blinding.

Thankfully, out of the corner of her eye, she spotted Carlos at the kitchen door with Dina and

Babs. They looked more like proud parents than bakery employees. They blew her a kiss.

The older woman was there getting her morning coffee. Kiki said she'd seen her at the Bakery Barn protest. She thanked the woman, who gave her a big hug in return. "Thank *you* for saving our Daisy's!"

The usual crowds were back, edging in and out of the door. That warm, electric hum was going again, radiating right through Kiki like a sunbeam. Daisy too had an orange-pink glow, and that feeling of connection enveloped Kiki like a cloud. She felt so relieved. Getting involved in the war of the bakeries had been the grand experiment of all time. And Kiki couldn't be happier with the results.

One of the *Don't Desert Daisy's Desserts* T-shirts had been signed by about a hundred customers and was now framed behind glass. It was hung in a prominent space on the wall. It would be a reminder of why everyone loved the place so much.

"Pssst!"

Kiki and Jesse heard Carlos at the back, motioning for them to come into the work area. They hustled over.

"I'm so glad you're here," Carlos explained. "I have been working on something special just for you, Kiki."

"Wow," Jesse's eyes got really wide. "It smells amazing in here. Like …"

"Baked love," Daisy said, patting Jesse on the back. "Carlos, did you show them? It's all he's talked about this week. In the midst of all that crazy, Carlos worked on a recipe for you."

"For me?"

He lifted a lid off of a cake dish and revealed a cake unlike any cake Kiki had ever seen.

"It's a rainbow!" Kiki said.

"Not just any rainbow," Carlos explained. "Remember when we were playing around in the kitchen the other week? We talked about the science of cooking, and then you told me a bit about how you were reading that *Charlie and the Chocolate*

Factory book?"

Kiki nodded.

"You said the Everlasting Gobstopper had to be the coolest invention *ever* – like a crowning moment in science. If it really existed, that is."

"That whole book just makes me drool, it all sounds so good!" Jesse said.

"Yeah, we'll call it Jesse and the Saliva Factory," Kiki laughed. "But you're *our* Willy Wonka, Carlos!"

Carlos laughed. "Well, I took Wonka's challenge and tried to imagine a cake that would showcase just how extraordinary *you* are, Kiki. Something that would bring in the science and the playfulness and – yes – the many flavours of the Everlasting Gobstopper. Well, sort of."

Kiki's eyes went wide. "What *is* this?" she asked.

"It's an Everlasting Rainbow Cake. It might not last forever, technically, but it has a lot of colours and flavours that make a flavour symphony in your mouth! Try a piece."

Jesse reached in with his fork first, but Kiki

pushed him away. She wanted the first magical bite.

Her piece had all the colours of the rainbow – and a different flavour for each colour. It was divine. Somehow Carlos had made them work together. The chocolate stood alone and then it became creamy coconut and then orange and lemon cream and vanilla and blueberry. Kiki's mouth exploded with flavours. Jesse dived in with a second fork and took his own bite.

"You should bring this cake into Mr Galipeau as your reaction recipe!" Jesse exclaimed.

"Yes, this is it! I've been thinking and thinking and couldn't decide on the perfect one, but this is definitely it. You'll have to teach me how to make it!" Kiki wanted to thank Carlos, but she wasn't sure how. She wasn't even sure what she was thanking him for. Was it cake? Was it *magic*?

Daisy stood off to the side, arms crossed. "You like it?"

"Are we allowed to have seconds?" Kiki asked.

Daisy laughed. "Of course! I can't thank you

enough for all you did these past days and weeks. You're part of our family."

"You're one clever cookie, Miss Kiki Booker!" Carlos cheered.

Kiki beamed, overwhelmed. She couldn't think of anywhere she'd rather be than right here, licking those multi-flavoured rainbow cake crumbs off her lips, standing next to her best friend, and enjoying the new friendship of everyone in the bakery.

"Can I get some of this cake to go and the recipe?" Kiki asked, relieved that she now had the perfect thing to complete her kitchen science assignment.

Some things couldn't be explained by science. Like how people she just met a few weeks ago could suddenly be so important to her. Or how a really tough science contest just happened to give her three baking questions she knew hands down. Or how wearing a T-shirt to support a small business somehow helped her dad with his big business project. But it didn't matter. It only mattered that in the end, everything turned out okay.

Now there was only one thing left to do: Get this ginormous rainbow cake home so she, Mum, Dad, Auntie Pat and Shawn could eat every last crumb of it together.

Back to the blog

Home
Meet the bakers
Recipes
- Cakes
- Cookies
- Tray bakes
- Breads
- Gluten free
- Vegan
- Dairy free
- Other

Archive
- January
- February
- March

Hello Sweeties,

I'll keep it short and sweet this week: Friendship matters more than anything.

As some of you know, Daisy's Desserts has been open for a while now, and in that time we've faced some construction issues, one broken oven and the arrival of a bakery superstore in a neighbourhood close by. But somehow, we have persevered! Thanks to all of our customers for being the sweetest part of our business. The recent "Don't Desert Daisy's Desserts" campaign showed us how much you care.

This month, tell a friend about Daisy's. We promise that the baked love will come right back to you if you do! Our community knows how to work together. And I'm here to work for you ... and to offer a little icing to sweeten up your day!

xo, Daisy

p.s. Special thanks to our good friend Kiki. She showed me that if people believe — really believe — anything is possible. She also was just awarded a special academic science prize by her school. Congratulations to her and to all the other scientists-in-the-making. Well done! Bring your certificates of achievement by and show me how well you've done this term — and you'll get a free treat from Daisy's.

Kiki's rainbow cake

Turn four small cakes into a rainbow layer cake extravaganza, Kiki-style! Make sure you use your maths skills to divide and measure when you bake. The best bakers are maths whizzes too.

Ingredients:

Large mixing bowl
Plain vanilla cake mix (mixed)
Four small bowls
Food colouring: red, blue, yellow, green
Baking spray
Four disposable round cake tins
Platter for display
2 tubs white icing

Directions:

1. Preheat oven to 170 degrees Celsius (Gas mark 3).

2. In large mixing bowl, follow mix directions to make cake mixture, but do not bake.

3. Divide mixture equally into four small bowls. Add a drop or two of one food colouring into each bowl so each bowl is its own colour. Stir each bowl.

4. Spray each of the tins and pour one coloured mixture into each tin.

5. Place all four tins into oven and bake for 10–15 minutes. Cake is done when you can poke a toothpick into centre and it comes out clean.

6. When cakes are cooked and cooled, carefully remove each one from its tin.

7. Place red cake on platter and ice the top. Place yellow cake onto iced red cake and ice the top. Repeat with blue and green cakes.

8. Once all four are assembled, ice the exterior.

9. Slice into the layer cake for the best rainbow effect!

Bonus: For some extra rainbow fun, add rainbow sprinkles all over the iced cake!

Meet the bakers

Daisy

Owner of Daisy's Desserts! With a frizzy head of magical red hair, sunny disposition and a treasure trove of recipes passed down from her dear Nana Belle, this always-optimistic baker is ready to serve you! Along with her crazy baking team – Dina, Babs and Carlos – Daisy aims to transform our city neighbourhood with sugar, spice and everything nice. From custard tarts to cupcakes, Daisy always seems to have the recipe for "baked love" up her flour-dusted sleeve. Inside Daisy's Desserts, the impossible somehow becomes iced with possibility!

Dina

Baker and waitress Dina specializes in sweets, especially when it comes to her personality! Designated mother hen of the crew, Dina not only has a way with a rolling pin and a whisk but also with our customers! She is always suggesting new recipes and encouraging Daisy to try new ingredients from around the globe.

Carlos

Daisy's number-one confidante and trusted sidekick in the kitchen, Carlos has a twinkle in his eye and pep in his step. A family man with four sweet-toothed children at home, Carlos is always inventing and testing new recipes in the kitchen of Daisy's Desserts. He is the master mix-man — to date, he's invented cookies, cakes and even Daisy's line of sweet treats for dogs. His favourite saying is, "I keep experimenting until I find the right formula!"

Babs

Like a Hollywood starlet from another era, Babs is always dressed to impress with a bouffant do and an apron to match every shade of lipstick. Our wisecracking baking beauty has a lingo all her own, calling customers "peach" or "sugar" before sneaking them samples of Daisy's latest baked goodies. Babs is also our bakery's guardian angel — years ago, she was BFFs with Daisy's Nana Belle.

Talk it out with Daisy!

Be brave! Sometimes that's easier said than done, according to Kiki.

Have you ever felt "in over your head" or scared you were going to fail?

How did you get through it?

Is there something different you'd do next time?

What encouragement would you give a friend who needed to be brave?

Good friends can help you through life's challenges. Come up with some examples in the story where you see evidence of good friendships. Then think of a time in your life when you were a good friend or someone was a good friend to you.

About the author

Laura Dower worked in marketing and editorial in children's publishing for many years before taking a big leap to the job of full-time author. She has published more than 100 children's books, including the popular tween series *From the Files of Madison Finn*. A longtime Girl Scout leader and Cub Scout leader, Laura lives with her family in New York, USA.

About the illustrator

London based illustrator Lilly Lazuli has a penchant for all things colourful and sweet! Originally from Hawaii, Lilly creates artwork that has a bright and cheerful aesthetic. She gains most of her inspiration from travelling, vintage fashion and ogling beautiful cakes. She enjoys making eye-catching artwork that makes people smile.

the Dessert Diaries

Friendship is the best recipe!

Year 7 pupil Emme is always trying to keep the peace. But when her parents decide to split up, and her BFFs get into a major fight, Emme finds herself caught in the crossfire. Can the opening of a new bakery help Emme to find peace again?

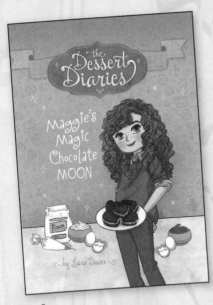

Maggie's Magic Chocolate MOON

by Laura Dower

Starting at a new school in Year 7 isn't easy. And the reason Maggie's at a new school is even worse. On top of it all, Maggie's little sister is driving her crazy! But when Maggie stumbles upon a unique bakery in her new neighbourhood, life starts getting a little sweeter.

Gabi isn't just allergic to peanuts, she's allergic to attention of any kind. But when her artistic talent is needed on a project to help her school, Gabi knows she has to step up. Suddenly, with the help of her best friend, a new boy and a beloved baker, Gabi's quiet world gets a sugar rush!

Gabi and the GREAT BIG Bakeover

by Laura Dower

For MORE GREAT BOOKS go to

www.raintree.co.uk

The Beating of His Wings

Paul Hoffman is the author of four previous novels, *The Last Four Things* (2011), *The Left Hand of God* (2010), *The Golden Age of Censorship* (2007), a black comedy based on his experiences as a film censor and *The Wisdom of Crocodiles* (2000), which predicted the collapse of the world financial system.